Murder on the Page

Book 2 of the
Harley Hill Mysteries

Kennedy Chase

Monty's Tale Press

Copyright

Acknowledgements

Big thanks to Mimi Strong and Pauline Nolet whose help
and advice is always greatly appreciated.

Kennedy Chase Titles

Harley Hill Mysteries

Book 1- Murder on the Hill
Book 2 - Murder on the Page
Book 3 - Murder for Christmas

Prologue

My name is Harley Hill, and I'm in serious trouble. *Again.*

Honestly, it's becoming a habit.

This time, I've been kidnapped. My hands are bound behind my back. I have a black sack over my head, and all I can hear are voices outside of the room, discussing how best to dispose of my body.

So far, the options are: being fed to dogs, thrown into the Thames with heavy shoes, buried in Epping Forest, sold to suppliers of kebab meat (*Ew! I'm never eating a kebab again*), burned in an incinerator, or, and surprisingly generous of hardened criminals, donated to medical science.

Who knew criminals could be so supportive of the sciences?

Of those choices—that is if I have a say in the matter, which I doubt—I think I'd go for being buried in the forest.

Despite being a city girl, there's a circle of life thing going on there, with my body giving the soil nutrients and whatnot so that a tree might grow.

In reality, I'd probably become the hiding place for an enterprising squirrel's store of nuts. Even that would be better than going into a kebab. I'm pretty small; I don't have a lot of meat on my bones and would make a rather disappointing meal.

To make matters worse, I'm stuck in this room with Alex Cobb, the ex-husband of my business partner, Cordelia Silvers.

Alex is a detective, and quite often a giant pain in the butt—despite him being terribly handsome. To be fair to him, it wasn't really his choice to be here. He was just trying to do the right thing and convince me not to break into the private club of the local Mafia family.

Given that we're now stuck in this unidentified room, bound and hooded, I assume he now regrets trying to do the right thing.

Not that he can tell me, being knocked unconscious.

He should have just arrested me. Although, if he did that, I wouldn't have gotten the proof I needed to solve a murder and a centuries-old search for a diary. A tome that would shake the world's establishment to its foundations.

Having the proof was one thing; being alive to use it was another.

But I'm getting ahead of myself.

All this started six days ago. I need to go back to the beginning to explain how all this came about. And hopefully, somehow, find a way out of this predicament before Alex and I are dog food.

Chapter 1

Day One

Two months after meeting Cordelia Silvers for the first time, I'm now in business with her.

To give you a very brief summary, I was kind of a rogue and in massive debt to an international crime lord.

My boyfriend, Cole Lockland (I'll come to him in a moment), knows Cordelia's ex-husband, Alex Cobb. He works for the police and flips between being infuriating and useful. Being incredibly handsome—and knowing it—only adds to his difficulty. He has charm, and knows how to use it.

Cordelia, along with her aunt, used to run a finders agency. They specialised in sourcing items for private individuals and companies. One of their main tasks was to find items for theatre and film sets. As well as the reverse: auctions and collectors would hire them to find props from famous films, costumes, and the like.

When I met Cordelia, she hired me to help with a small job that turned into quite a murder mystery—

which we totally solved, like bosses.

With that little adventure, not only did I manage to pay off my debt to the crime lord, but I also helped Cordelia settle her divorce with Alex so she could keep her house, the HQ for the business.

We launched it as Silvers & Hill Finders Agency.

So there's where we are now. We received our first job request a few days ago and just got a confirmation they were happy with our quote.

As for Cole Lockland… that's kind of tricky.

For years I had known him as part of the criminal underworld, but I always knew there was something different about him. For a start, he was a modern-day Robin Hood, stealing from thieves in order to return items or their cash value to their victims.

It was through Cole that I managed to start my life again as Harley Hill. My real name is Samantha, though I never use that now. I grew up through the foster care system, not knowing my parents or my siblings.

Cole helped me with a new ID and introduced me to Cordi.

It was shortly after that I discovered Cole wasn't all I thought he was. Turns out, he's an undercover cop. Not only was he working outside of the law to give justice to the people of London, but he was also working *with* the cops to bring down some of the world's biggest criminals. Oh, and I kinda love him, like a lot. After years of skirting around the issue, we eventually hooked up. So that's now a thing, perhaps, I don't know, it's complicated.

But let me cut to the new job Cordi and I had taken on, as from that day things got weird. Dead bodies kind of have that effect.

***

We arrived at The Page Foundry, a bookstore specialising in antique books, at ten-oh-five a.m. according to my limited edition Disney Swatch watch.

We had walked from Cordi's place in Notting Hill to here in Westbourne Grove—a fantastic road for those in need of retail therapy.

Fun fact: before this place was so affluent and 'up and coming,' it was an area controlled by notorious slumlord Peter Rachman. Oh, and if you're in the area, I'd highly recommend visiting Ottolenghi's and trying one of their flour-less chocolate teacakes.

They are to die for!

From the outside, the old bookstore looked like something right out of a Victorian-period drama. The woodwork was painted a deep red. Gold lettering spelling out the store's name adorned the large multi-panelled window.

Behind the glass, an elaborate display of old books caught the eye. On the large sign above the window, faded wording said the shop had been established since eighteen forty. I didn't doubt it. It looked quite out of place sandwiched between all the trendy furniture stores and clinical fashion boutiques.

We entered to a cheery door chime and the overwhelming smell of old paper, leather, and the mouth-watering scent of espresso coffee. It seemed our client had prepared for our visit. I liked her already.

A large lady, mostly held in place by a stretched canary yellow trouser suit, squeezed her way down a set of narrow stairs to the left of the store. "Cordelia, darling, so good of you to make it. And, Harley, nice to meet you again," she said, beaming a wide smile.

"Bethany," Cordelia said, holding out her hand. "Thanks for seeing us on short notice. We're eager to get all the details on this book you wish us to find."

Bethany Galbraith was one of two partners who owned The Page Foundry. She was in her late fifties and wore her striking grey hair in a bun atop her head. She wore bright make-up to match her trouser suit. Her cheeks were blushed with salmon pink.

Given the dull colours of the store, with all its black, green, and wine-red leather-bound books, not to mention the dark wooden shelves and stacks, she cut a striking, almost neon, vision.

"Let me just lock up and we can discuss the book in question," Bethany said, striding across the bookstore and locking the door. She flipped over an open-closed sign and returned to us, gesturing through a narrow doorway. "Come through to the reading room, I've got coffee and cake," she said.

She blustered her way expertly around a large table stacked with academic books of some considerable age. I read a few of the spines as I passed. They were nineteenth-century biology books. *Impressive. Expensive.*

But all I cared about right then was the word *cake*.

The reading room was super cosy. It was at the rear of the store. An eight-panelled window let in the autumnal sunlight, giving it a golden glow. Half a dozen old oak desks sat in a circle. Around all four walls of the room were more shelves sagging under the weight of hundreds of old books.

A wheeled book cart to the far right of the room overflowed with a jumble of publications, presumably awaiting the correct filing. On the opposite side, a snack bar had been laid out on a dark wooden table, above which hung a series of antique world maps in gold-gilt frames.

"Wonderful room," I said, following Cordi to a table. We sat down at Bethany's gesture.

"Thank you," Bethany said. "It's my favourite place to read. In the morning we have a robin that sits on the fence outside. It's a great place to wake up and enjoy a nice coffee before the bustle of the day starts."

Considering how empty, and quiet, the store was, I wondered just how much of a bustle there would be here. I can't imagine antique books are on everyone's daily shopping list.

Beth joined us at the table, placing down a pot of coffee and a trio of china cups. They were probably worth more than all my personal possessions combined.

A plate of cakes quickly joined us.

"I hope you like carrot cake," Bethany said gleefully as she stared at the confection.

I reminded myself I was in polite company and thanked our host before selecting the smallest piece. I nibbled at it, resisting the urge to stuff the whole slice into my mouth at once.

Oh my! It was so good. The flavours burst onto my tongue. Its texture was light and velvety. For those few seconds, nothing else mattered. I was in cake heaven.

"Wow," I said after finishing it. "That's some seriously good baking. Did you make these yourself? If so, can I have the recipe?"

Bethany's face lit up as she laughed. "No, my dear, despite my figure, I'm utterly useless in the kitchen. I bought these from a sweet old lady who has just recently started selling her cakes. Her name is… let me think. It was Margaret something… no, no, Maggie Le… oh, I can't remember it now, it was French sounding. I'm afraid the stress of this job is getting to me, scrambling my old brain."

"Leroux?" Cordi asked as she finished her slice.

Bethany slapped the table. "Yes, that's it. You buy

from her too?"

"Not quite," Cordi said. "She's my aunt. I didn't even know she was going into the bakery business. She used to be my partner, but although she baked for us, she never made anything as delicious as this. Seems she has improved considerably."

I couldn't believe it. Cordelia's crabby aunt, 'Aunt Maggie', was now selling her cakes. I suppose now that she wasn't working in the agency she had more time on her hands. She certainly was a mysterious one.

"What a coincidence," Bethany said. "Small world!"

"So, about the book?" I prompted, wanting to get on with things. I was eager to hear more about this book that we were supposed to find. "Can you tell us more about it? Anything you have learned that would help us track it down."

"Of course, dear, of course. First you'll want this." Bethany rummaged in a large purse by her feet and pulled out a CD in a plastic case. She slid it across the table. "I took the liberty of typing up all my notes and having my business partner, Graham Simpson, burn the files to disc. He should be here by now. He's probably got his head in his books again..." Bethany looked off into the store, her forehead creasing with concern.

I took the CD and placed it in my biker's jacket inner pocket. "Thanks," I said. "I'm sure this will be helpful."

Bethany stood from the table and poked her head through to the store as though she were listening for something. She returned with a fake smile. "I think Graham must have got distracted in the vault."

"Vault?" Cordi asked.

"These old buildings have huge basements," she said. "For many years our basement was used as a vault back in the eighteen hundreds. We had it adapted to store rare and expensive books and papers. When we first set up in business, a benefactor of a large private library, Henry Constable the Third, donated his collection of over twenty thousand items to Graham. Ever since then, Graham has made cataloguing and researching that collection his life's work."

"I imagine that's going to take quite some time," I said.

Bethany rolled her eyes. "If he stopped being so stubborn and let others help him, he would have had it done years ago, but he refuses. He wants to do it all himself. I swear he spends more time down there than he does in his own home. Which probably explains why he's still a bachelor at sixty-three."

I had to admire that kind of dedication.

It must be nice, I thought, *to have a life's work to spend your time on.* I'd never really had a calling or a burning desire to do just one thing. I've spent most of my life drifting around, trying my hand at one thing or another.

Perhaps that's why I decided to settle down and work with Cordi—to build something that I could truly care about. Foundations, I suppose. We all need foundations to build our life on, whether they are made of family, hobbies, work, or charity.

"Well," Cordi said, "while we wait for Mr. Simpson, would you like to tell us about the book?"

"Indeed, sorry, I'm terribly distracted this morning." Bethany took a deep shot of coffee. "I'll start at the beginning—feel free to interrupt with questions."

Cordi and I took out our notebooks and waited for Bethany to start.

"Graham first came to know about the book during one of his research sessions on the private collection," she started. "He found a series of mentions of a 'Doomsday Diary'. This isn't to be confused with the Domesday Book; that's a separate thing. The diary is reputed to have belonged to the seventeenth-century philosopher John Dee."

I gasped. "As in the aid to Queen Elizabeth the First?"

"The one and the same," Bethany said with a glint in her eyes. "Although this 'Doomsday Diary' is different to the currently available diary of John Dee, the latter being mostly concerned with his daily business of the time. It's an interesting historical record in its own right."

I was stunned. I had read about John Dee when I was at school—*before I got expelled*. For some reason, I developed a fascination with him. He was one of the first true polymaths, excelling in astronomy, mathematics, and alchemy among other esoteric topics.

"So what's in this diary of his?" I asked as Cordi scribbled notes.

"That's the crux of it," Bethany said. "In the two mentions of this book that Graham has discovered, it talks of great occult revelations, but more importantly, secrets on the royal family and many of Dee's patrons of the time. People like William Cecil, Christopher Hatton, and others. The passage talking of this diary comes with a dire warning: if the book was ever to come to the public's attention, it would shatter the establishment to its very core."

Cordi and I stared at each other in silence for a moment, taking in the gravity of the situation. I didn't like the sound of the occult revelations anymore than the shattering of establishment.

I was no fan of the Royals, but if this book was as potentially explosive as Bethany said, then there'd be many people who would want to stop the book from seeing the light of day.

Bethany continued on, filling us in on the details. "The book is rumoured to have been sold into a private collection shortly after Dee's death around sixteen-oh-nine. He had one of the largest private libraries in England at the time. Many of those books were sold off to various prior patrons and other interested parties. Most were recorded and accounted for. But in all our research we can find no other record of this Doomsday Diary."

"Do you know for certain it exists?" Cordi asked. "Could the passages Mr. Simpson found be inaccurate?"

"He'll certainly tell you no. The passage came from a journal entry of an unimportant librarian in the early eighteenth century. Every other book mentioned in this list has been located or corroborated in other collections and libraries. The Doomsday Diary, however, has not."

"So how much is this book worth?" I asked.

Bethany took a deep breath. "My dear, the Doomsday Diary, if found, would be worth a third-world country for the revelations alone."

That I didn't like—something that valuable would surely bring a lot of interest. "How many other people know about this book?"

"As far as I know, it's just us and Graham," she said. "He has kept this secret until we brought you two in. Hence the contracts he demanded you sign along with your quote."

"Could we speak with him?" I asked. "Does he have a cell phone on him? We could come back later."

"He doesn't have a cell phone, I'm afraid. He's far too old-fashioned for that. You'd get a quicker response sending a carrier pigeon. I know, seeing as he hates me going into the vault, why don't you go down there and see if you can convince him to surface. I'm sure you'll get a response out of him, being such a pretty young thing."

I was about to decline, not wanting to be stuck in a vault with an old hermit, but before I had a chance to speak, Cordelia said it would be a great idea.

Thanks, Cordi!

Bethany stood and took me by the arm. She led me through the store until we came to a steep set of stairs going down into the basement. I really didn't like the idea of being 'sexy bait' for an old bachelor.

Besides, I was hardly wearing glamorous clothes, just my usual everyday uniform of skinny black jeans, biker boots and jacket, and an old Deep Purple band T-shirt. Cordi would be a better choice, with her curvy figure decked out with a beautiful floral-print Laura Ashley dress and winter suede boots.

With Bethany's powerful presence behind me, I felt like I had no choice but to go down there. I resisted the prickling sensation of fear and stepped down into the vault.

"The light down there isn't great," Bethany said, handing me a flashlight. "Best use this until you reach the back room. Graham will no doubt be at his desk, hunched over a book by lamplight. Tell him we have a new stock of ginger biscuits if he doesn't initially come with you."

Great! I felt like a child-snatcher trying to lure a kid

with the promise of cookies.

Bethany had turned her back and retreated into the reading room before I had a chance to say that I didn't want to go into the creepy basement.

Annoyed at myself, and Bethany, I switched on the flashlight and ducked below the small doorway, descending the cold, stone steps into the dark.

A terrible chill coiled around my exposed neck.

The place was thick with the stench of old, rotting paper.

All around me were walls made from stacks of boxes, inside of which were innumerable books and papers. I guessed this was the private collection Bethany was talking about. The wall of boxes created a narrow passageway going left.

I followed it around, the damp air making my skin turn to gooseflesh. I wasn't even ten feet into the darkness when I kicked something on the floor. I swung the flashlight down to see what the dark shape was...

And let out a yelp of a scream.

Lying there, staring up at me, was an old man in a brown three-piece suit, clutching a leather-bound journal to his chest. His mouth was wide open as if he were silently screaming. His lips were a dark grey colour. Brown eyes in shadowed sockets stared into the far distance, giving him a haunted expression. His chest didn't rise or fall. A gold pocket watch, attached to his suit jacket, was in pieces by his side as though stamped upon.

I bent down and tentatively touched his hand. He was as cold as the stone floor.

That's when I ran.

Chapter 2

When Detective Alex Cobb turned up at The Page Foundry with the rest of his squad, the first words out of my mouth were, "It wasn't me!"

Alex gathered us into the reading room while the CSI team dealt with the body.

He didn't look happy; this was the first time he had been in the same room as Cordi since their divorce was finalised a few weeks previous.

Bethany was still sobbing in the corner of the reading room, dabbing at her eyes with a handkerchief. Her mascara had run down her face. She looked a mess.

As bad luck as it was having Alex be the detective on the case, I *was* glad to see him.

He was pretty good with the whole commiseration thing. Partly because of his ridiculous levels of charisma, but also because despite him being an annoying arse most of the time, he was genuinely good at his job.

"I need to take your statements," Alex said to Cordi and me after a liaison officer consoled Bethany. "Start from the beginning and don't leave anything out."

Cordi sighed, not hiding her irritation. "We've

already told you everything, Detective *Cobb*," she said, emphasising his last name to reiterate their separation. She turned away from him and poured another coffee from the pot on the snack bar.

"She's right," I said, looking up into those gorgeous eyes of his. Although I was with Cole, there was still something about Alex that caught my eye. He resembled a younger Harrison Ford. "There's little else to tell. We came here to discuss a job, and when I went into the basement to find Mr. Simpson—I, well, found him."

Alex sat casually at the table, notebook in hand. He stared into my eyes as though trying to draw out my very thoughts. "And you didn't notice anything or anyone else in the store or the basement? No noises or anything like that?"

"None," I said. "I went down there and literally walked into him." I shuddered with the memory of those dead eyes staring up at me. "As soon as I realised he was dead, I sprinted back up the stairs and told Bethany and Cordi what I had seen."

"Why is it that whenever I run into you, you're at the centre of trouble?"

I shrugged. "I guess trouble likes pretty young things."

"Trouble isn't the only one." Alex flashed me a quick grin. His cheeks dimpled, and I had to look away. That smile was like a tractor beam.

"So what now?" I said. "You want us to go down to

the station?"

"I don't think that will be necessary. I'll wait until the CSI guys have finished assessing the scene, though. It's not like you two are going to skip town anytime soon, are you?"

"I doubt it," I said. "Bethany still wants us to find this book. It's become a point of reason now. For Mr. Simpson's legacy."

"Well, that's good," he said. "Perhaps we'll run into each other again, but I'll warn you now, and this goes for Cordelia too—I don't want you getting involved with trying to find the murderer, *if* this is murder. That'll be *my* investigation."

"You say that, but who was it who cracked the case last time?" I said. "That'll be me."

"And who was it who saved you from being killed by that very murderer?"

⬚Touché, detective douche.⬚

"I mean it, Harley, I don't want you to get in over your head like that again."

I looked away from him. Bethany had finally got a hold of herself and was talking with one of the uniformed officers, who took notes. Cordi was standing with her back to the old maps on the wall, her hands around a mug of coffee.

"You sound like you care," I said. "You should be careful about that. It'll ruin your reputation."

"Oh?" Alex said, raising an eyebrow. "And what

reputation is that?"

"For being a total arse."

"Hey, I work hard to cultivate that reputation. It's not easy, you know."

"Well, you certainly make it look easy."

Alex stifled a laugh and flipped his notebook closed. He approached Cordelia and talked with her in hushed tones.

Cordi avoided his eye contact and answered his questions.

I stood up and stretched my legs. I couldn't get the image of Mr. Simpson's dead eyes out of my mind. That image would stay with me forever. And that feeling… the coldness. At least I now knew what a dead body felt like.

If 'touch a corpse' was on my bucket list, I could emphatically strike that one through.

An hour later, they took Mr. Simpson's body away. Bethany broke down in tears again at the sight of his still form.

Alex said he'd be in touch soon with an update on the investigation.

When the store was quiet once again, Bethany locked the doors and returned to the reading room. "The robin's back," she said. "That's unusual. He normally only sticks around for the morning."

I watched the bird stare into the room as he chirped and flittered on the fence. I wanted to say something about him paying his respect, but I didn't want to set her off again.

She looked worn out with all the crying. She sat heavily at the desk, slumping her ample bosom on the surface. "I can't believe he's gone," she said. "He's just always been there. I don't know what I'm going to do now without him."

"I'm so sorry," Cordelia said. "Is there anything we can do? Do you have friends or family you can be with for a while?"

She looked at both of us with a renewed steely determination. "Find the diary," she said. "It's the least we can do for him. That was his ultimate goal."

"We'll do it," I said with gusto, wanting to give the woman the confidence that we were up to the task. Although I wasn't entirely sure we'd be able to find this book. It had been missing for over four hundred years. "We'll get started right away." I patted my pocket, indicating the CD with her notes. "Would you like us to call anyone for you?"

She shook her head and smiled wearily. "You're a sweet girl, thank you, but I'll take responsibility for that. Graham had little family; it won't take long to inform them—if they'll even care. He wasn't one for staying in touch with people, you see. He loves his books more than people. They are… were… his entire world."

"We'll do our utmost, I can assure you of that," Cordi said.

Bethany shook her hands and showed us out of the store, thanking us again for agreeing to take on the challenge.

I breathed a deep sigh of relief to be out of there.

The fresh air filled my lungs, clearing out the dust of the old books.

"That was intense," I said as we headed back down the road toward Cordi's place.

"Yes, quite the upsetting experience. Poor Bethany looks heartbroken. I hope she'll be okay. I'll check in on her in a day or so to make sure she's doing all right."

"I'm sure she'd appreciate that."

"So," Cordi said, "what's on your plan for the rest of the day?"

I knew why she was asking this. When we had finished our last job, she had surprised me by finding an address for one of my siblings—my brother. For the last two months, I've had the card in my purse. I've stared at it every day since, trying to decide if I should go and see him or not.

I've never met any of my siblings. I had no idea if he would hate the idea of me just dropping into his life. I'm not sure I could take the rejection.

"I know, I know," I said. "But it's not easy."

"I understand. But if you don't go and see him, you'll never know. You did say today was going to be the day."

"But what about Mr. Simpson and the book? We need to work on that."

Cordi stopped in the middle of the street and turned to me. Pedestrians washed around us, tutting and huffing. "Listen, I need to go and speak with Maggie to find out what she's up to. This is the second time I've heard of her selling cakes to businesses. Besides, finding books and things is something she can help with. While you're going out to see your brother, Maggie and I will start to draw up a plan of action for this Doomsday Diary."

"Fine, I'll do it, even if it just means I can forget about it and move on."

This wasn't something I entirely believed. Whether I was accepted or rejected, moving on wasn't something that I felt would be as easy as all that.

We continued to walk down the street until we came to the tube station. I said goodbye to Cordi and headed southwest. My brother lived in the leafy suburbs of Wimbledon.

I tried to call Cole on the way, but for the third day running, there was no answer. I refused to leave another message. And refused to let his silence get to me.

Yeah, right.

My guts were all twisted up with not knowing what was going on. The last time we were together we had some seriously good sexy times after a romantic dinner.

Everything seemed perfect.

Then he had to leave on business, not saying whether it was Prince of Thieves' business or undercover cop business. Seriously, guys, if your girl gives you a great time, call her soon; it's not too much to ask, is it?

I put my worries about Cole behind me and stepped on the train.

A horrible feeling of dread made my legs wobbly, but it had to be done.

Chapter 3

The train stopped at Putney Bridge station and I got off. The platform is actually over ground here. The sun was shining, but it did nothing to warm me up. I still felt the chill of finding Mr. Simpson's body.

Or perhaps it was just the fear of finding my family.

A suited man bumped into me and told me to get a move on. I realised I was standing still, looking at the station exit, my travel card in my hand.

"Sorry," I muttered and willed my legs to move.

I followed the dozen other travellers out of the station like a zombie and hurried over the crossing to get to the other side of the road. I stopped and looked back, wondering if I should just forget about it and focus on the Doomsday Diary.

The station was forbidding with its beige brick frontage and huge arch. A group of grannies sitting at the bus stop looked at me with casual interest. I felt like they were judging me. Telling me I was a chicken.

I'll show those grannies! I turned to face the road and walked with purpose toward my brother's address. The terraced townhouses here are about as expensive as those in Notting Hill—mostly because of its close proximity to the Wimbledon tennis facility and the Common.

Cars were parked on both sides of the street.

My brother's place was about halfway down. Number thirty-four.

I counted down the numbers, each one making me more nervous. I was on the opposite side of the road, so when I reached the right spot, I had to look across the road to the house. His one was painted a light yellow colour.

Outside was a top-of-the-range, metallic silver Lexus. He obviously did okay for himself, job-wise, given the property prices and the expensive car. I wondered what he did. Maybe he worked in the city as a broker or perhaps an advertising exec?

I was about to step across and knock on the door when I saw movement behind the wide, bay window. A large conifer tree in the front garden shadowed the front of the house, making it hard to see.

The door opened and a man stepped out with two small girls behind him.

They couldn't have been more than about three or four years old. He had them all wrapped up with hats and scarves to protect them from the crisp air. They were smiling and reaching their little hands to the car, excitement clear on their cherubic faces.

The man—my brother?—opened the door and got

them settled into child's seats in the back. He was a fairly handsome man, standing over six foot, with a wide, athletic frame that was showing the beginnings of a paunch. He wore jeans and a black polo shirt beneath a sports jacket. His hair was thinning at the temples and crown, and he'd shaved it close.

I guessed he was in his early forties. I never knew when my sisters or brother were born. I only had one photo of him.

When I was just a young girl, someone had delivered a photo to me with the words 'You're not alone' scrawled on the back. The image showed me as a baby with my three sisters and my brother. In the photo he must have been a teenager or in his early twenties.

And here I was, nearly twenty years later, staring at a man I barely recognised, wondering if I had got the wrong place or if Cordi's research was wrong and this wasn't my brother at all.

Without realising what I was doing, I found myself stepping across the road toward him. He looked up as he reached the front of his car. We locked eyes for a split second, and I *knew* it was him. I could see my own eyes looking back at me.

I froze and everything seemed to go in slow motion. He was saying something to me, but I didn't hear his words. The girl in the nearest seat looked at me and raised her little hand.

And then he was moving toward me.

He dropped his keys and bag and was running forward.

I didn't understand what was happening until he grabbed me around the waist and pushed me back across the road with his momentum.

I tripped on the curb and fell backward. He collapsed, but rolled away as we both hit the pavement. And just like that, the world came rushing in like a flood.

A car horn blared and its engine revved. A blur of red flashed by, just inches from where I just stood.

A shadow loomed over me. "Are you okay?" he said, panic in his voice, sweat glistening on his face. He panted for breath and held out a hand.

I took it. He lifted me to my feet.

"You could have killed yourself," he said. "Didn't you hear me warn you? What the hell were you doing just standing there in the road?"

The words wouldn't come. I had no idea what to say. This man, my brother, just saved my stupid life.

"Are you deaf?" he asked, doing that slow exaggerated speech so that I could read his lips.

"No," I finally muttered, rubbing the back of my head. "Sorry, I can hear you, thank you... for..." I became dizzy and my legs gave way. He reached out and stopped me from falling. I dropped the card with his address on and staggered back.

"Easy," he said. "Just take some deep breaths. You've had a shock."

The shock wasn't just from nearly being run over. It was discovering that my brother was a courageous man. Even hearing his voice blew me away. It was like for the first time I realised there was more than just me in the world. I *did* have a family, and he was standing right here, holding me steady.

Embarrassment made me blush. I stood up straight and squirmed from his grip. "Thanks," I said, "I just had a dizzy spell. I've not eaten much today, probably low blood sugar. I completely zoned out. I didn't even hear the car."

"Well," he said. "No harm done. Are you sure you're okay? Did you want to sit down for a moment? I could call someone…"

"No, really, thank you, you've been kind enough."

We looked at each other for a moment. I wondered if he could see the resemblance in my eyes. I was wearing a lot of black eyeshadow and mascara, and my black fringe covered my eyes somewhat.

"If you're sure," he said, looking back to his two girls in the car. I could tell he wanted to get away from the *crazy woman*. I was still wearing my black skinny jeans and boots. Along with my biker's jacket I probably looked like trouble to someone in these parts.

"I'm sure," I said.

"You've dropped something," he said, bending to pick up the card. He made to hand it over to me but must have read the words on the reverse side. He brought his attention back to me, his eyebrows meeting in the middle as he tried to figure out what was going on.

"Are you here to see Mercy?" he asked. "My wife."

I didn't know what to say. I couldn't lie and say yes, but if I said no, how could I explain that I had his address? In another time, I'd have come up with an amazing lie off the top of my head, but the stress of the situation robbed me of my wit.

"No," I said, "I was just…" I couldn't say it. I panicked again, snatching the card from his hands and running away up the road toward the train station.

I didn't stop until I reached the platform. Bending over and resting on my hands on my knees, I caught my breath and watched to see if he followed.

No one came. I didn't expect him to; he had his children to look after anyway. Assuming they were his, they'd be my nieces. Tears flowed, and I slumped down on a bench, waiting for the train.

I had a family and they were just a train ride away!

And yet I couldn't say anything. I couldn't tell him who I was, too scared he would freak out and refuse to have anything to do with me. Given he was in my old photo, he must know that I exist, and he, along with my three sisters, had never made any attempts to get in touch.

A bored teenager was watching me. I wiped my tears away, hoping I didn't look like Bethany with my mascara running all over my face. At least with my clothes I could pretend I was paying homage to Alice Cooper.

My phone rang. Initially I was going to ignore it with the stupid idea that it was my brother. Of course it wasn't, how could it be? My number wasn't on the card. I checked my phone. It was Cordi.

I composed myself and answered. "Hi, Cordi, what's up?" I asked, trying to sound like I had myself together. Cordi didn't buy it for a second.

"You sound upset, what's happened?"

"Damn, woman, are you psychic or something?"

"My mother was a witch," Cordi said, making me laugh. "Seriously, what's up? How did it go with your brother?"

"Urgh! The worst. I'll explain when I get back. It was kind of a disaster."

"Oh, love, I'm sorry to hear that. I'll have some chocolate cake ready for when you get back. In the meantime I have some news from Alex about Graham Simpson."

"I'm listening."

"They got a toxicology report back. They're saying it was suicide. He poisoned himself with arsenic. Apparently, he'd drunk enough to kill half a dozen people. They're not treating it as suspicious."

This didn't sit right with me. "They came to that conclusion pretty quickly. It's only been what, six hours since they took the body away? Have the police ever been that quick before?"

"It's hard to say. But Alex thinks something's up. His superiors reassigned him to a non-homicide case even before it was confirmed as a suicide. Apparently, he says there was a lot of tension at the station. Something's definitely not right."

"Old boys network covering something up, you think?"

"I wouldn't rule anything out right now. I spoke with Bethany, and she doesn't buy it either. She said Graham just wasn't the kind. Although he lived like a hermit, he wasn't depressed. He loved his work. Lived for it, she said. So she's asked us to look into it. She seems to think it's related to the book."

"Oh great, killer on the loose after the Doomsday Diary; that's all we need."

"She's doubled the fee."

"Oh, in which case, count me in. Okay, my train's here. I'll see you shortly."

I hung up and jumped on the train.

Although Mr. Simpson's death had taken a terrible turn that would likely put Cordi and I in danger, the excitement of the development helped take my mind off my brother. For now at least.

As I sat on the train, something sharp jabbed into my left boob.

Checking my inner pocket, I found that the CD Bethany had given to me had shattered into a number of pieces. It must have broken when I fell over the curb.

Damn it! I hoped Bethany had another copy; I could have just seriously delayed our investigation.

And with the fee doubled, that would turn out to be a costly screw up.

Good job, superstar!

Harley strikes again.

Chapter 4

When I entered the Coach & Horse, our old-fashioned local pub, my heart sank.

Cordi's aunt Maggie was here. Sitting opposite Cordi within a booth.

It looked like she was berating Cordi about something, wagging her finger and shaking her head. Her white hair, done up with curlers, wobbled with each word. She wore a bright pink cardigan over a pale blue blouse. The colours clashed horribly. But that was Maggie's style—I had seen some of the clothes when Cordi cleared out a room for me.

I wondered why so many old people were eccentric. I supposed it was because by the time you got to that age, you didn't really care what people thought, and you just wore whatever you were comfortable in or whatever was clean at the time.

I kind of envied that kind of freedom.

"Hey, Harley," Cordi said, standing and letting me into the booth. The shiny leather of the seats from thousands of previous buttocks made it easy to slide in.

"Hi, Cordi," I said.

The pub was pretty empty at this time of the day. It was late afternoon, and it would be a while yet before most of the patrons got off work and came in for dinner and a few pints.

"You look like you've been crying, girl," Maggie said, scrutinising me with her grey eyes behind thick pink-framed specs.

As doddery and eccentric as Maggie seemed, she was far more observant than she let on.

"It's nothing; I just tripped over at the train station. Nothing a brandy won't fix."

"Coming right up," Cordi said, taking the opportunity to get away. "Oh, and Auntie, why don't you fill Harley in on the information you found out about the book while I get the drinks."

"Make mine a sweet sherry," Maggie said.

"Of course," Cordi said, moving to the bar.

"So you've been doing some research?" I asked to get things going.

Maggie just nodded and smacked her lips together as though she hadn't heard me. I was about to speak up when she looked me square in the face. "That scoundrel Cole Lockland hasn't upset you, has he?"

"Huh? No… it's…" I was about to say 'none of your business,' but I just looked down at the table and shook my head. "He's fine," I said, which of course was rubbish. I'd barely heard from him, and every day that went by, I got more worried about him.

About us.

"That's the face of someone who has had a man hurt her," Maggie said, pointing one of her gnarled, crooked fingers. "I've seen that look a thousand times, most of them from Cordelia. But then Cole Lockland is no Alex Cobb."

"No," I said, my voice quieter. "He's not."

I wasn't enjoying Maggie pulling on a raw nerve and was going to ask her about the book when she interrupted me, as if sensing my thoughts.

"I spoke to some friends of mine," she began, "in the baking club I belong to. A couple of them are historians and knew Graham Simpson. I had one of them look up this Doomsday Diary. At first I thought it was a load of old hogwash."

"But you found something out? Something that would help us find it?"

"Not quite. But I know that it does exist. And perhaps something that can give you girls a lead."

"Oh? Go on, tell me more."

Maggie leaned closer and looked around to make sure we didn't have company. Cordi was still waiting to get served. Even though it wasn't busy, they only had one bartender.

"Gerald, my friend, is an expert on these things. The diary used to be considered a myth. At first it was mostly known through word of mouth, but over the years, a number of publications and other personal correspondence were discovered that proved the diary did exist."

"But nothing to say where it might have gone?" I asked, hoping we'd have at least some lead to go on.

Without reading Bethany's notes, so far we had nothing.

"Well, not quite, no, but something we can work on. After John Dee died, it was rumoured that the diary was given to a close friend of his as protection against those who had opposed Dee and Queen Elizabeth. Dee had recorded many hundreds of secrets on both the monarchy and dozens of lords, earls, and parliamentarians."

"So it was like an insurance policy?" I said.

"Quite," Maggie replied, smiling her weird little smile and exposing her crooked teeth. "Dee was an exceptionally bright gentleman, but because he was so close to Elizabeth, he also drew a lot of enemies. He rightly knew that information was power. It was that information that would keep him alive for as long as he was, and later, his close friends and fellow scholars."

"So we're still hundreds of years away in that line of enquiry," I said. "It could have gone anywhere from there. Do we know what happened to this friend?"

"Murdered in cold blood by a particularly nefarious earl."

Maggie's face lit up with this. She seemed the type of person who enjoyed reading violent historical books.

The Elizabethans weren't exactly known for their delicate approach to conflict.

"And do we know which earl this was?" I asked.

"We don't," Cordi said as she came back to the table and handed out the drinks.

"Thanks," I said, taking the brandy. I swallowed deeply, enjoying the warmth as it went down.

I sank into the seat and sighed, letting all the stress of meeting my brother flow out of me. By the time I finished the drink, I felt a lot better and was starting to think more about the diary.

"That's not entirely true, Cordelia," Maggie said.

Cordi sighed. "Okay, Auntie, give us your theory."

This seemed to light an inner fire within her. Her eyes shone brighter, and after she had finished her sherry, she rubbed her hands together as she told us her theory. "The earl could be one of many, but he's not that important in the grand scheme of things."

"Then how will we trace this book through history?" I asked.

"If you give an old girl some silence, I'll tell you," Maggie said, scrunching her face up with a slight cackle.

I sat back and listened, suitably chastised.

"It all starts with what's in the diary," Maggie said. "We know it included secrets, but more importantly, it's rumoured to include some of Dee's more outlandish theories about magic."

I knew a little about this from my school days.

John Dee believed that through maths and other sciences he could eventually divine the one true language and commune with the angels. Many people considered him a magician due to his knowledge of astrology, divination, and alchemy. He had made it his life's work to uncover the universal language of creation.

He was one of the few people of the time to consider magic and science the same thing, and sought to use this theory as a way of understanding the divinity beyond the physical world.

"How outlandish?" I asked, risking another deadeye stare from Maggie.

"His work to commune with the angels was just the first step in his goals," she said. "He went a lot further in his theories. Are you familiar with Aleister Crowley?"

"Of course, he was a little cuckoo, right? Thought he could speak with the devil and stuff?"

"Something like that, but if my research is to be believed, some of Crowley's ideas match some of those from Dee's more wilder theories." Maggie stopped and watched me as though waiting for me to come up with the point of this information.

"Are you saying that the diary went to Crowley?"

Maggie shrugged. "Maybe, maybe not."

I was getting tired of her games. I wished she'd just come out and say it. She seemed to enjoy playing with us, using her extra knowledge as a power game.

Cordi urged her to continue. "Get to the point, Auntie. We've still got work to do today."

Maggie put her hands up and sighed. "Okay, okay, everyone's always in a rush these days. Fine, the book is likely to have gone to an obsessed fan of Crowley's. With the help of my historian friend, we found mention of these theories of Dee's a number of times in various occultists' books. There's a common word that seems to connect all of the mentions."

"Which is?" I prompted.

"Heruda."

I shook my head. "It means nothing to me. What is it?"

"Beats me, you'll have to find that out yourself," Maggie said. "But I have a lead for you. My friend is pretty good on that interweb thing."

"Internet," Cordi said.

Maggie waved away her correction. "The Heruda occult group have been around for nearly twenty years. They're based in London, and some of their doctrines and theories resemble some of those by this obsessed fan of Crowley's."

"So," I said, piecing it all together. "You think that the diary made its way down the years to a number of occultists, and is now with a group called the Heruda?"

Maggie nodded. "Could be a complete dead end, but it's the only connection we've got. You'll really need to read Mr Simpson's notes to see if there's any more clues."

"We have the CD," Cordi said. "We'll check that out when we get back home."

"Um, about that," I said, wincing as I explained what happened.

Maggie gave me a withering look of disapproval, but Cordi tried to make me feel better, as she always did. "We'll see if Bethany's got a copy. In the meantime, I have another lead on Mr. Simpson's death."

"Wow, you two have been busy! I feel like a slacker," I said.

"Oh, I'm sure you've been busy too. We'll have a catch-up later when we're home."

In other words, when Maggie wasn't here to eavesdrop on my personal affairs.

"So tell me about this lead," I said.

"We're going there shortly, actually," Cordi said. "We've got an appointment to speak with a Mr. Cheesebury."

"Who?"

"The owner of The Page Foundry's competitor, The Book Vault," Maggie said. "He's a stuck-up simpleton with delusions of grandeur."

Cordi rolled her eyes. "He unsuccessfully courted Auntie once."

"And now spends his time breathing in paper mould," Maggie responded.

"Huh, who knew there'd be two such places? I'm

assuming they didn't get along?" I said.

"They used to once," Cordi said. "Charles Cheese-bury was pleasant enough on the phone. I had originally called him to ask if he knew Graham Simpson, in order to find out if the latter had any enemies. Turns out, Cheesebury *is* such an enemy."

"No way, what was their beef?"

"He didn't say. He was worried that the police were tapping his telephone. He said we have to speak in private, as he's worried he'll be framed for the murder."

"But the police said it was suicide," I added.

Maggie shook her head again. "My friend at the baking club who knew ol' Simpson said he'd never top himself like that. For one, he was a coward and a hermit and wouldn't say boo to a goose, and secondly, he was closing in on finding Dee's diary. Why would he kill himself now when he had a new life's mission? He was extremely driven, by all accounts."

"So we're definitely treating this as murder, then?" I asked.

Cordi nodded. "When I spoke with Bethany, she's convinced the diary and the death are related. It might not be, but you have to admit, the timing's suspicious."

I spun my glass on the table's surface, watching the light from the wall lamp swirl in the dregs. I made Cordi right—it did seem suspicious. But for other reasons too.

There's no way the police would work that fast and rule it as suicide. There had to be something else going on there that we didn't know about.

Cole might know something, I thought. I wanted to call him again, but after getting no response for days, I couldn't handle the rejection of hearing it go to voice-mail once more.

"When do we speak with this Cheesebury?" I asked.

"We can go now," Cordi said. "By the time we're finished talking with him, we'll have time to drop in on Bethany and see if she has a copy of that CD."

We got up and walked to Cordi's old Mercedes.

Maggie got in the back, and Cordi dropped her off at her place in east Notting Hill before we turned back and headed for The Book Vault in a little village in Surrey, just outside of London.

Despite my problems with Cole and my brother, I felt good again about being on the mystery trail with Cordi.

I just hoped that Mr. Cheesebury would have something useful for us.

As it turned out, he would have more than something useful.

Chapter 5

We stepped out of Cordi's car and crunched across the gravel of the car park.

All around us, oak and beech trees created a red and brown autumnal blanket. The air was chilly and I shivered, clutching my leather jacket closer.

I regretted not having brought a scarf or a thick sweater.

We came to a narrow passageway between terraced buildings and into the high street of the village. To our left and at the top of a hill was an old church; the clock's hands told us it was approaching four p.m.

To our right, the high street stretched out with shops, cafés, and pubs lining the two sides. A few hundred or so people milled about, breathing plumes of air.

"Quaint place," I said.

"Ideal location for a historical bookstore," Cordi replied, consulting a page of notes. "It should be just around here."

We followed the directions and turned right into a side street at the corner of a café. It had the most amazing smell of pastries and coffee wafting from it. "If we have time, I'd like to get a pie or a cake on the way back," I said, trying not to press my face to the window and drool at the two grey-haired ladies eating a scone with jam and butter.

Cordi grabbed me by the arm. "Come on, don't scare the wildlife."

"I *am* the wildlife. Especially if I don't get some food in me soon."

"You never know, Mr. Cheesebury might take a fancy to you like he did with Auntie and ply you with snacks."

"Are you suggesting I offer myself out for confections?" I said, stepping around a little old man who had for some reason just decided to stop in the middle of the street for no apparent reason.

He looked up at me with bushy eyebrows and a scowl.

"You really ought to time your outbursts," Cordi said, sniggering at me as my cheeks blushed. "But no, I wasn't suggesting you prostitute yourself for a donut, just use your charms a little."

"We'll see how good looking Mr. Cheesebury is," I said, nudging Cordi with my elbow.

"Here it is," she said, pointing to a corner unit.

The Book Vault was in better shape than Bethany's store.

A royal crimson canopy hung over the front of the store, the name embossed on the cloth with bright silver lettering. The windows were clean and bright with a number of books—both ancient and modern—on display. I was pleased to see he had the latest Stephen King and J.D. Robb titles in.

"Ooh," Cordi said, standing in front of the window, pointing. "He has the new Agatha Christie editions. I've been meaning to fill out my *Poirot* collection."

"I had you down as a *Miss Marple* fan," I said.

"That's more Auntie's taste."

"That figures. Oh, looks like we've got company."

I gave Cordi another nudge, and we entered to a distinct lack of cheery door chime.

Strike one against Cheesebury.

A tall, gaunt figure in a dark three-piece suit hovered in the middle of the store like a praying mantis. His large eyes turned to us. A thin slit of a mouth smiled in what I can assume was a welcome, though it could quite well be the look of someone who has just really enjoyed passing wind.

I nervously smiled back, avoiding his steely gaze.

While he crept along the floor to greet us, with a pronounced limp, I got a good look at the place.

Unlike The Page Foundry, this store was cosy without the smell of rotting paper.

Twenty-foot-long bookshelves lined both sides. Where they ended, a set of dark-wood steps led up to a second, carpeted level. There, it looked more like a small library with a dozen rows of stacks, each one dedicated to a different subject or genre.

Like the window display, there was an even mix of old and new. He even had a Young Adult and Children's section.

A couple of elderly ladies were browsing the titles at the back in the Mystery & Thriller section while a younger man, wearing a *Metallica* T-shirt, was studying the books in Science Fiction & Fantasy.

I know it's odd, but it was really nice to come into a bookstore that didn't smell of coffee. It seemed these days that all the chain stores on the high street were now a quarter bookstore and three-quarters coffee outlet. Not that I didn't like coffee, but I liked the purity of the store being dedicated to just books.

"Ms. Silvers and Hill, I presume?" Cheesebury said, holding out his skeletal hand.

Cordi smiled and shook his hand. "Thanks for seeing us, Mr. Cheesebury."

"Please call me Charles. If you'd like to follow me in to my office, I'll be happy to answer all your questions. It's such a terrible business what happened to poor old Mr. Simpson."

Before we had a chance to retort, Charles was spinning on his heel, his back ramrod straight. "Millie, dearest, would you mind looking after the place for a moment? There's a lamb."

A teenage girl with a messy curly mop of blond hair poked her head above a stack, her arms buckling under the weight of books. She wore an old-fashioned dress and long socks. She looked a student from *St. Trinian's*.

"Of course, Mr. Cheesebury," she said, feigning a smile. The poor girl rushed to place the stack of books on the floor and turn to the two older ladies, who were asking about something.

"Follow me, ladies," Charles said as he limped up the stairs and entered a door on the rightmost side of the store. His office was opulent, to say the least. Rich, red velvet curtains hung over a large window to the rear. A huge, mahogany desk with green lamps and a leather blotter dominated the room.

In the far corner I spied a painting of a fox-hunting scene. I guessed from the orientation of the walls that's where he kept his safe.

Behind and to the left of the desk was one of those drinks globes.

"Please take a seat, ladies," he said, stepping around his desk. He bent to the globe and flipped the lid to display a wide variety of spirits. "May I get either of you a drink? I have a particularly fine cognac that a good friend of mine brought back from Italy."

"Thanks, but I'm driving," Cordi said.

He raised an eyebrow and lascivious smile toward me. "Ms. Hill?"

"No, thank you, but thanks for offering."

"Then I hope you don't mind if I help myself. It's all been quite unpleasant these last couple of days. Bethany's been beside herself with grief."

"I'm sure it must be quite the shock for everyone," Cordi said.

While they made their obligatory politenesses, I looked over his desk with disinterest. I noticed a well-thumbed Sudoku puzzle book opened to the difficult pages, and one of those executive toys with the row of silver balls on wire.

I couldn't resist and pulled back the first ball.

"Oh no, Ms. Hill, please don't—"

Too late.

The ball struck the row of others. To my horror, they all fell from the wire and bounced in all directions off the desk. They rolled off the edge and onto the floor.

Feeling embarrassed, I jumped out of my chair and chased them down. As I dashed to my left to stop one ball from rolling under the desk, my foot came down on another and I slid back with surprising speed.

My weight fell forward, unbalancing me.

Pinwheeling my arms for balance, I struck Charles in the face with the back of my hand, slapping him with a loud crack.

I fell forward and reached out with my other hand. I crashed into the drinks globe. It toppled over, spilling its contents on the thick, ornate rug beneath. I clattered into the mess. My legs tangled with Charles', making him lurch forward.

The glass in his hand followed the momentum. As

did the ice and cognac.

It splashed right down onto Cordi's head, flattening her hair and dribbling down her face to soak her dress.

She jumped out of the chair with shock and head-butted Charles in the chin with the crown of her head. Both Cordi and Charles yelped and staggered back.

After some effort I managed to stand. "Oh my! Are you both okay? I'm so sorry!"

Cordi looked at me wide-eyed. At first I thought she was about to tear a strip off me, but then she just looked down at herself, then me, and burst out with laughter.

I couldn't help but join her—even as I put the bottles back into place.

Charles stared on with fury in his eyes, but even he, with his top button done up and his tie pulled tight around his scrawny neck, saw the funny side. He then left the room and returned with a towel for Cordi, who took it and dried herself.

He shook his head and sat down behind the desk. "I hope you're not hurt, Ms. Silvers," he said. "And I'm sorry about your…" He wagged a finger at her wet dress. Her bra was showing through, and Charles could barely take his eyes off Cordi's charms.

At least that was one way to get his attention off me—and what I just did.

Cordi rubbed the top of her head. "Just my pride, Charles, just my pride. Is your chin okay? I really whacked you hard there. I heard your teeth snap shut."

"Nothing a trip to the dentist won't fix," he said, with that creepy smile of his. He fixed his glare on me, adding, "Ms. Hill, please don't worry about the mess. I'll get it cleared up later."

"I'm really sorry about your balls," I said. "I didn't realise they were broken." Even as I said the words I knew how it sounded.

Cordi bit her fist to stop herself from laughing further.

Charles simply nodded his head once and regarded some invisible lint on his suit. "With that little episode over, please ask your questions. I'm happy to help."

I coughed, composed myself, and waited for Cordi to start off.

"On the phone, you mentioned that you had a long-standing business problem with Bethany and Mr. Simpson," Cordi asked. "Could you elaborate?"

"Of course," Charles said. "I didn't want to go into it further—you never know who's listening in these days. Um, but yes, the issue… Well, it started about five years ago, during the recession. The Page Foundry was starting to find itself in a bit of a financial pickle. With Mr. Simpson spending most of his time in his basement cataloguing the private collection he was given, the running of the business was mostly left to Bethany."

"I see," I said, scribbling some notes. "So was there animosity between the two regarding this?"

"In a word, yes." Charles steepled his fingers and

placed the tips on his chin as he considered his words. "Mr. Simpson was a peculiar old fruit. He'd rather live in that dingy basement of his, surrounded by old books, than actively help the business through the hard times."

Cordi picked up on that and pressed further. "Do you know the extent to these hard times? Were they in trouble as a business?"

"They… well, Bethany still is." Charles cleared his throat and continued. "The crux of the issue was that Simpson was a stubborn bloody fool. I had offered them a cash injection for a percentage of the business. This would have enabled them to buy in some modern stock, create a website so people could search their antique titles, and get the place modernised so it didn't feel like a damned tomb every time you stepped inside."

"And they didn't take the offer?" I asked.

Charles looked genuinely annoyed when he replied. "No, Simpson and his damned pride refused the offer. He thought I was trying to muscle in on the business— to get closer to Bethany. The silly old fool was always jealous of me. Just because Bethany and I go back years to when we were kids. We grew up together, you see. I only wanted the best for them. Unlike Simpson, I didn't view us as competition. But rather as allies against the march of the chain stores with their terrible coffee and even worse snacks. Bethany and Simpson grew apart with no small matter of animosity between them."

I made some notes about Charles' body language. His shoulders were tight and he balled his hands into tight fists as he recalled the story.

"So, Charles," I said, "what happened after he refused? Their store is still going, so they must have come through the recession even without your cash injection."

He shook his head and snorted. "Only because of Bethany's savings. She's propping that place up herself. That poor woman had to do everything while that fool Simpson hid in his horrible little basement like a cockroach. She was at her wits' end and becoming ever more desperate. With him stalling her at every turn, she was becoming quite desperate."

"How long can she continue like that?" Cordi asked, pulling her blazer jacket closer together to stop Charles' attention from flitting back to her chest.

"Well," he said, his eyes becoming shifty. "I guess you ought to know. You'll probably find out during your investigations anyway. Bethany told me she'd hired you two to follow up on Simpson's ridiculous treasure hunt."

"And his murder," I added.

His eyebrows flew up like arches, making him look like a startled owl. "Murder? Whatever gave you that idea? It was suicide. Plain and simple."

"Quite," Cordi said, skipping over that little outburst as I continued to note his reactions down. "But tell me,

Charles, what ought we to know?"

He unclenched his fists and rubbed his hands together. With a heavy sigh, he came out with it. "For years Simpson refused my help. The business was a partnership between him and Bethany, so she couldn't accept my money without his agreement. But now that he's... let's say out of the picture, Bethany is now the sole owner of the business and has agreed to accept my original offer. Sadly, because it's ruled as a suicide, she won't get any life insurance. Other than his collection, he had nothing to leave in his estate."

"What about his family?" I asked.

"He didn't have any. His damned collection and this myth of the Doomsday Diary were the closest thing he had to family. Or at least that's the way he acted. I don't know who hurt him so much to turn him into such a recluse."

"I hate to ask such a blunt question in these circumstances, Charles, but where were you yesterday at the time of Mr. Simpson's death?" Cordi asked.

I was expecting more of a reaction from him, given his clear disdain for the deceased, but without missing a beat, he replied, "I was at a private collector's house. I arranged to procure some of his books for the store."

"Is there someone who can vouch for that?" I asked.

Charles reached into his jacket and pulled out a card. He handed it to me across the desk. "Gavin O'Reilly, the collector. He'll confirm I was there. And I believe he has a security camera looking at the front of his building. I dare say he'll have me on video arriving and leaving."

"Thanks," I said, placing the card into the interior pocket of my notebook.

"Charles, just one more question," Cordi said. "Then we won't take up any more of your time, you've been entirely generous already."

"Please," he said with that smarmy smile of his, "ask away."

"I notice you don't have a wedding ring. Do you have a partner?"

"As a matter of fact, not that I see the relevance of the question, no, I do not. I'm a bachelor and a respected one at that."

"No offence intended," Cordi said. "I just wondered, with you and Bethany having so much history together, and now business partners, if you two were perhaps a couple."

"Absolutely not," he said, standing up. "Beth is a very dear friend. Now if you don't mind, you've taken enough of my time. I'm going to have to ask you to leave."

He swept around the desk and opened the door. He stared at us expectantly.

Cordi and I wasted no time and left the store. We made our way back through the town until we got to Cordi's car. We got inside and talked about Charles' reactions.

"Quite the odd fellow," Cordi said. "Although it's all very interesting about this cash investment business."

"Does somewhat give Bethany motive to kill her partner, doesn't it? No estate as such, but getting Simpson's half of the business and the investment from Cheesebury I'm sure would be very motivating."

"If we hurry, and the traffic isn't too bad, we might make it back to Bethany's in time. Fancy another shakedown today?"

I grinned. "Absolutely, as long as you don't mind going there in your current state."

"I've had worse. Besides, this case is just starting to get interesting."

"Let's do it, then."

Cordi fired up the Mercedes, and we headed back to The Page Foundry. I felt excited to find out what Bethany was going to say.

This could be a definite step forward in the case.

Chapter 6

By the time we arrived at The Page Foundry, it was already dark. The high street was pretty much deserted, the staff and shoppers alike having left to go home for their dinner.

Pools of yellow light spilled out onto the streets from behind the windows of the shops. A diesel-engine bus rumbled up through the road. Black cabs swerved around it and sped off into the distance.

My teeth chattered together and the chilly early evening air blew into my face, nipping at my nose and the tops of my ears. I put my hands in my pockets and huddled down into my jacket. I reminded myself I'd need to get a scarf and a thicker coat soon.

"Looks like we're late," I said.

We stopped outside Bethany's. Unlike the other shops, hers was in darkness. I could just about make out the glow from a street light at the rearmost part of the store. It shined through a narrow gap between the doors that led into the reading room.

"What should we do?" I asked. "Come back tomorrow?"

Cordi scrunched her face. "She did say she would be here. Perhaps she's up in Simpson's apartment. I imagine she's got a lot of paperwork and whatnot to sort out. I'll call her."

Cordi rifled through her pocket of paper scraps, trying to find Beth's number.

While she was doing that, I noticed movement inside. Stepping closer to the window, I saw a shadow stalking around the displays of books. Then there was a small, narrow beam of light. I knew that when I saw it: a flashlight.

"Crap, Beth's being burgled," I said.

I instantly thought about Simpson's private collection. What if this burglar was going to steal the something on the Doomsday Diary?

I checked the door. It was open. The thief hadn't locked it behind him—obviously making sure they had a quick exit. But it also meant I had quick access.

"Wait, Harley—"

I didn't hang around to listen. My muscles tensed and I slipped inside, using all the cunning and stealth I'd developed over the years in my shady past.

My eyes quickly adjusted to the gloom.

The burglar was hunched over and making their way around the large table of academic books, heading for the vault. Their flashlight swept around the store and up the sides of the walls. They were definitely looking for something.

I was just ten feet away, crouching behind them.

That's when I launched myself, diving over the book display, and tackling them around the waist. My momentum drove them into a stack of books.

The unit crashed to the floor, spilling its literary contents.

"Ow!" the burglar cried as a heavy tome hit them on the head. They struggled, but I knocked the flashlight from their hands and pinned them to the ground, leaning my weight on them.

What now? I thought. I hadn't really considered what I would do next.

I didn't have a chance to think, though. The burglar struggled beneath me, and then I heard a cell phone ring. It was coming from the intruder.

"Get off me," the voice said.

Huh… that wasn't right. It sounded like…"Bethany?" I asked.

"Yes, now get off me, whoever you are, I'll call the police!"

Her cell phone was still ringing, and when she struggled to pull it free from her pocket, the light illuminated her face—it *was* Bethany!

I quickly got to my feet. "Oh crap, I'm so sorry," I said. "I thought you were an intruder…"

Cordi rushed in after me, her cell phone in hand. She looked at me aghast when she realised I had taken Bethany down like an amateur rugby player.

"What are you doing in the dark?" I asked. "I thought you were trying to rob the place."

She reached up her hand, and I took it, helping to pull her considerable frame to her feet. "The fuses tripped. I was coming down to reset them."

"Your door was open," I said in defiance.

She sighed. "I know; I hadn't yet locked up. I was about to do that when you attacked me like some lunatic. Do you have a habit of just charging into places like that?"

I shrugged. "It's been known."

"We're so sorry, Bethany," Cordi said, placing her phone back into her jacket pocket. "We didn't mean to do… well, this. Are you okay?"

She rubbed her head. "I took a knock, but I'm sure I'll live. What are you two doing here, anyway? Wait, before you say another word, let me reset the breakers… as soon as I can find that damned flashlight."

I had seen it roll to the side. I bent down for it, just at the same time as Bethany, and we banged heads. "Goddammit!" Bethany said.

"Ow, I'll just stand back before I do anymore damage," I said after seeing little stars bloom in my vision. I rubbed my head, easing the pain as Bethany eventually found the flashlight and made her way across the store.

She opened a cabinet door and reached inside. With a splutter and an electrical hum, the lights flickered on, making me squint in the sudden change of light.

"That's better," Bethany said. "At least now I can see you coming for me."

I thought it was a joke, but she wasn't smiling. I didn't blame her. I'd just wrecked her store. "I really am sorry," I said.

She brushed it off. "Now, what can I do for you both? Is there any news on the diary?"

I gave Cordi a raised-eyebrow look. Odd how the woman was more interested in the diary than any leads on her partner's death—which she herself suggested was murder. These weren't the actions of someone who cared about her old friend and ex-business partner.

"We have a few leads," Cordi said coolly, not giving anything away. "But we hoped you might have a backup copy of that CD—I'm afraid the disc was corrupt and we couldn't get anything off it. Probably just a faulty disc from the pack."

I appreciated Cordi covering for me like that—especially as it was my own stupidity that had broken it. The whole scene with my brother came flooding back; I felt the burn of shame and embarrassment return as fire in my cheeks.

"I'm afraid I don't," Bethany said, bending down to pick up the books and placing them into neat piles. "Graham burned the disc on his laptop. I don't know anything about all that computer stuff."

"Is there any chance he might have a copy somewhere?" I asked. "Perhaps stashed in his vault?" I thought I'd try to get a sneaky few minutes in there to see if I could find any clues as to the whereabouts of the diary.

The basement door was covered with yellow police tape, and I noticed it had a brand new, and large, padlock keeping it secure.

Bethany shrugged. "It's unlikely. Even if he did, you'd never find it down there; the place is a total mess. He hadn't used any known filing system I could make out the last time he had allowed me in. It looked like a rat's nest with papers and books piled every which way. How he found anything in there is a mystery to me."

"Would you mind if we had a look?" Cordi asked.

Bethany stood upright and paused for a moment.

Her eyes squinted before she eventually said, "It's still a crime scene. I'm afraid I can't let you in, even if I could. However, Graham's laptop is upstairs in the apartment. I had kept it back when the police came by yesterday and took away some of his possessions. He had some contracts and things on there that I needed access to, and I didn't want them taking it."

Bethany chewed her lips for a moment, her hands on her hips. "I tell you what, if I give you the laptop, would you be able to get past his password-secured account? I have no idea what it is, and he never told me. I can't get into it, and I need those contracts."

"On that subject," Cordi said. "We just have a few

questions about Charles Cheesebury."

Bethany's eyes narrowed at that. Her large frame became taut in her bright orange trouser suit. "What do you know about Cheesebury and me?"

"Oh, that you and Mr. Simpson disagreed about the cash injection, and now that he's gone, you've accepted Cheesebury's offer," I said.

"What's that weasel been saying now? How dare he divulge our confidential information!"

"Is it not true, then?" Cordi asked.

"Well, I didn't say that. It's just… well, you can understand how it looks for me, can't you? It doesn't paint me in a good light, but it's just awful timing. The business is struggling, and if it wasn't for Charles, I'd have had to go bankrupt. Poor Graham's funeral expenses alone are going to make it difficult for me to survive—even with Charles' investment."

"Well, if you give us the laptop," I said, "I'll get through the security and perhaps we'll find the diary. If it's as valuable as Mr. Simpson thought, then all your money worries will disappear—and besides, I'd like to make sure you can afford to pay us for this job."

"Oh, don't worry about that. Your payment is guaranteed—that's already been set aside. Wait here and don't touch a thing. I'll go and get Graham's laptop."

I waited until Bethany had climbed the stairs and started to tidy up the mess I had created. As I turned to face the door, I saw movement outside. A shadow appeared at the window. Their hands were pressed against the glass, creating a funnel around their head as they peered inside.

It was a male with long black hair, dark skin, and sharp brown eyes.

We saw each other for a brief moment. When I blinked, he'd gone, his dark form already crossing the street.

I put it down to a customer just being nosey. The sign on the door said closed, but they were probably wondering why the lights were still on… but the way he looked at me… so intense.

The hairs on my arms prickled.

"Are you okay?" Cordi asked. "You look as if you've seen a ghost."

"I'm fine, really. I just thought I saw someone outside. But I guess it's just the bump on the head." I gave her a smile and continued to fix my mess as I waited for Bethany to return, all the while thinking about the guy at the window.

Who *was* he?

Chapter 7

Day 3

Not even the best coffee could wake me sufficiently. The previous night, I had battled with futile resistance against an army of yawns as I leaned, or more accurately, slumped, against Cordi's kitchen table.

At some time during the very early hours—or *late* hours, depending on which way you looked at it—I had finally got through Graham's user security. I was clearly losing my touch.

My friend in Tokyo, Henzo, would have got through it in seconds. He'd taught me a few things about information security a few years ago, but I hadn't kept up, or improved upon, those skills.

I wiped the sleep-dribble from my chin with my sleeve and popped the lid of the laptop. Windows loaded up, and I was staring at Graham's desktop wallpaper: a picture of John Dee, *naturally.*

The little clock in the task bar told me it was seven twenty-three a.m.

Cordi was still asleep. Her snoring rattled through

the entire house.

I stretched and reached for the pot of coffee only to find I had already drunk it all. It was then I remembered that during the early morning I had found the files that were burned to the CD.

Tracing my steps, I fired up the file explorer and tried to remember where the folder of information was stored. As I tapped away at the keyboard, running search strings, trying to remember how I found it before, I heard a heavy *thump*.

"*Mrow*," Monty, the great ball of fluff, said. He purred loudly, right next to my ear, his tail flicking behind him.

"Morning, fur ball," I said, scratching him behind the ears. He bopped his head against my face, and I got a whiff of his foul breath. "You really need some minty fresh gum, you know that?"

"*Mrow*," he retorted. I didn't know if that was agreement or a curse.

Probably the latter.

Monty finished rubbing against my face and turned around.

I leaned back so I didn't get a face-full of cat butt. He then decided the laptop keyboard was his new bed. He stepped on it, mashing the keys as he turned around in circles as though performing some weird cat ritual.

The laptop bleeped its protest, and various windows and files flew up on the screen.

I gently moved him off the keyboard and got a nip

to the hand for my efforts as he moved his great body away, jumping down to the floor and giving me the stinkiest of all stink eyes.

When I looked back at the laptop screen, I saw that Monty had only gone and opened the right folder. There before me was a dozen files, all titled with mentions of the diary.

"Who's a good devil-cat, huh? Yeah, you are, you're a good devil-cat."

No *mrow* this time; just a stare and a smug swish of his tail.

"Yeah, yeah, I know you're talented. No need to be so obnoxious about it."

While Monty did laps around my legs, I clicked into each file and read the information. There really wasn't much; most of it was just observations about Dee and conjecture as to the diary's whereabouts. It seemed it wasn't really worth burning a disc after all. But I suppose they didn't know what might be useful at the time.

But something else caught my attention. Something that wasn't in the files at all, but in an email that had popped up, presumably as part of the search result.

Cordi came into the kitchen, talk-yawning. "Morning, I feel like crap. Any coffee?"

"I'll make a fresh pot," I said, "but before that, I've found something very interesting."

"*Meow.*"

"Okay, *Monty* found something interesting. We ought to hire him out as an elite hacker. That cat of yours has some skills."

"He'd make a good scarecrow. Or haunted house prop."

Monty turned his nose up at Cordi and sauntered out of the kitchen.

"I don't think he took that too well," I said. "I'm sure we'll both pay a terrible price of retribution now."

"Not if I feed him tuna; it's his kryptonite."

"Good to know!"

"So," Cordi said, stretching her arms and smoothing down her crazy bed hair, "what have you and Monty found that has you so chipper at this awful time of day?"

"Perhaps a lead. The information that was on the CD really doesn't tell us anything we didn't already know. It's just stuff about Dee that we can easily look up— most of it's on Wikipedia."

"Wiki what?"

"An online encyclopaedia."

"Oh, I'm assuming this is something that I should have heard of by now?"

I nodded and gave her a sympathetic look. "Probably."

"When we have more time, you'll have to show me more about all this online stuff."

"Will do, but in the meantime, the lead I've found should give us something to work on. This string of emails is between Graham and someone who calls themselves *Dark Horse.*"

"They sound friendly," Cordi said, leaning over my shoulder and squinting at the screen.

"People use all kinds of names online. Mostly for anonymity so they can troll and abuse others on comments and social media."

"Trolls?"

"Don't worry about it; it's not important. You'll learn all this stuff eventually. Anyways, the conversation between Graham and DH is like something out of a John Le Carré book. Lots of cloak-and-dagger talk about a journal and secret meetings. They discuss the Doomsday Diary amongst other occult things."

Cordi leaned closer and started to read the chain of conversations, her lips moving silently as she scanned the words. "They're talking about a journal. Perhaps Simpson's personal one?"

"I've already thought about that. When I found his body, he was clutching a journal in his hands."

"Hmm, so that means it's either with Bethany or at the police station, locked away as evidence. I'll give Bethany a call, and you can brew a pot of fresh coffee. I feel like a zombie this morning."

"Consider it done," I said as Cordi left the room to find her phone underneath the detritus of her house. Even though it was better than when I first came, I still couldn't say that it was neat or ordered.

By the time I had made the coffee, Cordi came back into the room.

"Bethany hasn't seen it," Cordi said, her hair covered in dust and cobwebs.

"You know, we ought to invest in a cleaner once this job is done."

I pointed to the webs on her hair.

"Urgh, I guess you're right. The last thing I want to do is swallow a fly; then I'd have to swallow a spider and so on…"

"And we wouldn't want that; where would you find room for cake?"

"There's always room for cake. I have a special stomach-pocket reserved for such things."

We shared a smile. I was glad, because I was about to upset her.

"If Beth doesn't have it, then it must be with the police. I'm going to go over there and see if I can find it." This also meant I had to deal with Alex, Cordi's ex.

Her smile faded and she breathed out slowly. "Don't let him jerk you around. This is more our case now—more so with the suicide nonsense."

"Don't worry, I'll get the truth out of him one way or another. I have methods." I gave her a devilish grin. Her own smile returned and grew wider when I gave her a mug of coffee.

After taking a deep sip, she asked, "So what's the plan? We get Graham's journal and hope that gives us more of a lead?"

"Something like that. But while I'm over there dealing with Alex, would you mind going through all these files and emails to see if there's anything I've missed? Perhaps there's something that will help us find the identity of this *Dark Horse* character."

"Sure, if you show me what to do."

Despite Cordi's lack of experience with computers, she picked it up quickly and was soon clicking through Graham's emails and reading the files he had collated on the Doomsday Diary.

I left her to it while I went to get showered and dressed. I chose my standard outfit of black jeans, black T-shirt, and my leather jacket. Although this time, I borrowed a thick-knit scarf from one of the many boxes of film props in the spare room.

These were all gathered together by Maggie when she used to work with Cordi.

Despite the several layers of junk, there were some real gems in the boxes. The scarf, for example, was an extra-long, multicoloured affair. It looked like one that *Dr. Who* from the seventies might have worn.

I knew that if Cordi needed money in a hurry, she'd likely be able to sell a lot of this stuff for a decent amount. There was everything from *Star Trek* uniforms to accessories and hats worn by people on *Dallas* and other '80s soap operas.

Cordi was pacing the kitchen when I came back

down, feeling fresh and awake from the shower and change of clothes.

"Nice scarf," Cordi said. "It used to belong to *Dr. Who.*"

"I thought it did. I used to love watching that as a kid. That theme tune used to scare me though, sending me hiding behind the sofa."

"And don't forget all the terrible rubber aliens and wobbly sets."

"TV gold."

"Talking of gold," she said, sliding the laptop to face me. "Look what I've found."

I did a double take as I looked at a picture of a dark-skinned man with long black hair and intense brown eyes—the same one I saw last night outside The Page Foundry. He was wearing a thick gold chain around his neck. A pendant in the shape of a horse hung from the chain.

"Who is this?" I asked, though I already had a good guess.

"Our one and only Dark Horse." She pointed to the email in which it was embedded.

I plugged in the USB drive that I keep on my key ring and transferred a copy of the image over and then scanned the email.

It read:

DH,

So good of you to get in touch about the Dee book. I'm sure our association will bear fruit. With our joint efforts, we'll certainly discover its whereabouts. In the meantime, I've attached an archive of files on my work so far. I'm sure you'll find these interesting to you and your fellow Heruda followers.

I look forward to hearing your thoughts on my theory of its location. I'd like us to meet next week to discuss this in more detail... privately. We're getting close, and I don't want this getting out to others seeking the book.

May you ride the Horse in glory.

GS.

"Well, it seems like the Heruda are an equestrian cult of some kind. It's unique," I said. "I'll give them that."

"I looked in the attached archive," Cordi said, "but it was just more of the same: lots of theories of Dee's work with the angels and his attempts to communicate with them. His notes also suggest that he managed to actually find a way, and the Doomsday Diary, if used correctly, will bring about the pre-apocalypse of humankind."

"That explains its title, then. Do you believe in all that?" I asked.

Cordi shrugged. "I honestly don't know. I studied the bible at school in Religious Education class. At the time I believed it, but now… well, perhaps age has made me too cynical. I wouldn't rule anything out, though. What about you?"

"When I was in foster care, one of the families was Catholic. They used to take me to church every Sunday, but I didn't really care for it. I like the idea of there being an all-mighty supreme being, but I honestly don't know. I guess I'll find out when I'm gone."

"That's a grim thought for the morning."

"I'm sorry," I said, "I'm being a total Ms. Buzzkill. Do the archives say anything about the secrets Dee had about all those important people?"

Cordi shook her head. "None that I've found, but there's hundreds of email conversations. I'll get through them all eventually, so I'm sure we'll find something else. It does feel like I'm invading Simpson's personal life, though."

"But it's for a good cause," I said. "I'm sure he wouldn't mind us snooping if it means finding the book and his killer."

"I guess you're right." Cordi returned her attention to the laptop. "Oh, wait a minute, what's this?" Cordi sat closer to the screen and squinted. "I don't believe it," she added.

"What have you found?"

"These emails, the dates… there are a thread of them dated on the day of Simpson's death."

I leaned over her shoulder and scanned down the list

of emails.

Cordi was right.

It appeared Simpson and Dark Horse were talking via email just a few hours before we arrived for our meeting. "Open that one there; it's the last email in the conversation before Simpson died. The time says it was received at nine twenty a.m. Forty minutes before we got there. That's suspicious, no?"

"Certainly is, although it could just be a coincidence. But let's not rule anything out at this stage."

Cordi double-clicked on the message. It popped up in a new window. It was from Dark Horse and read:

Okay, GS. I'll be there before you open up. Make sure you have the journal with you, and I'll bring the money as a goodwill gesture. It's exciting times, my friend. I'm sure John Dee would be proud.

DH.

"Well, well," I said. "It looks like we've got a suspect. Perhaps once he had learned of what Simpson had found he wanted to find the diary for himself?"

Cordi pressed her lips together as she thought about it. "It's possible, but given the amount of emailing between the two, it seems like they were working together and had some kind of bond. I suppose we'll need to see what was in that journal before we can draw any conclusions. And let's not forget the journal was *with* Simpson after his death."

"You're right. We really need to find out what was in it. To Alex it is, then."

"Do you want to borrow the Mercedes to get to the station?"

"I'm good, thanks. I'll take the tube. I need to walk off this anxiety."

"Anxious about meeting with Alex?"

"Not quite, though it's definitely man trouble."

"Cole?"

"Yeah, that too, but also…"

"Oh, your brother? You never did tell me how that went."

With a sigh I told Cordi about the whole thing; how I nearly got run over, how he saved me from a certain death, and how I totally blew it and ran away like a scared schoolgirl.

"I'm sorry it didn't go well," Cordi said, wrapping an arm around my shoulder. "But there's always another time. I'm sure it'll be easier next time."

"*If* there's a next time," I said, not sure I wanted to meet my brother after all. He looked settled. I'm sure he didn't want something from the past just dropping into his life after all this time.

"At least have some carrot cake before you go off to see Alex," Cordi said, fetching a tin from the kitchen counter. "Auntie dropped these off yesterday while we were out."

"She's not so bad, you know."

"You've not had to live and work with her for all those years. Sure, she makes amazing cakes, but she'll drive you absolutely bonkers if you spend more than a few minutes in her company."

"Well, it only takes a few seconds to accept a cake," I said, grabbing a slice of Maggie's carrot cake. I chomped on it and said my goodbyes as I left to speak with Alex.

I had the familiar feeling of butterflies in my stomach as I walked down Portobello Road on my way to the station. At first I assumed it was because, despite Cordi's warnings about him, there was just something about Alex that made me feel like that.

Similar to Cole.

As I walked down the street, enjoying the bright morning sunshine—even if the wind was cold, but unable to penetrate my massive scarf—I checked my cell phone a dozen times, wondering if I should call Cole.

It'd been days since we last spoke, and my messages weren't being returned.

I knew he'd likely be at the station today. I remembered him saying he was working on a new undercover case, and today was the day he was meeting with one of the other snitches.

I wasn't sure if I wanted to see him or not. I was furious, yet I craved to hear from him. I hated the whole situation. I was starting to regret ever getting involved.

Men were just trouble in any which way you looked at it.

And I was about to walk right into the middle of more trouble—Alex.

Chapter 8

I approached the desk sergeant in the police station. He looked like a bulldog chewing a wasp with his bloated, stubbly face and short-cropped grey hair. His patchy complexion revealed he was the type to enjoy a scotch of five of an evening.

"What can I do for you, miss?" he asked, pen in hand, as if ready to jot down a confession.

"I'm here to see Detective Cobb."

"Name?"

"Hill, Harley."

"Is he expecting you?"

"Yes," I said, totally lying. I'm sure Alex would be intrigued enough that I was here to see me.

Without saying another word, Bulldog picked up a phone and dialled an extension.

I couldn't make out the conversation with his being behind a plastic barrier, but when he placed the phone back in the cradle, he nodded towards the blue plastic chairs.

"He'll be right through. Take a seat."

I avoided the temptation to salute him as I sat back

down and waited. A pair of scruffy kids sat opposite me. They were elbowing each other, leering at me. I rolled my eyes and looked away. Luckily, I didn't have to wait too long for Alex to arrive.

A door to the side of the reception area opened and *he* stood there, smiling.

"Ms. Hill," Alex said, charming and sincere. He'd clearly excelled in his public relations training since his promotion. "So glad to see you again. Why don't you come through?"

"Alex," I said, standing up, "I'm not here on personal business."

"Oh?"

"Can we talk somewhere private?" I asked as I walked through the door.

He smelled real good. His cologne made my nostrils flare as I took in his fresh, clean scent. It reminded me of days spent on the beach during the summer break from school.

"Follow me. I have an office we can use—unless you'd prefer an interview room?" he said with an arched eyebrow.

"Office will be fine, Detective Douchebag."

"I could have you arrested for insulting a police officer." He led me down a bland corridor, made only blander by the grey carpet. The police weren't really hot on interior design these days. I think they called this arrangement 'soul-destroying chic.'

"If you really want to be insulted, just keep pushing me. I've come here for your help, nothing else."

"You know I'm single now, right?"

He opened the door and gestured for me to enter. I waited for him to go in first and followed inside. I took a seat opposite a desk filled with papers and files. He sat behind it and cleared some space.

"Divorced—from my best friend and employer," I corrected.

"So? That doesn't stop us, does it?"

"You seem to be forgetting I'm with Cole now."

He just nodded and leaned on his forearms, staring at me with those piercing blue-grey eyes of his. I looked away, not wanting to get mesmerised by him. For all his faults, he was incredibly handsome, in a rugged, manly way, but I wouldn't let him get to me.

"So about this help," I said, handing my USB drive over to him. "Will you help me, even if it means helping Cordi?"

"It depends on what you want me to do."

I gave him a quick rundown of the situation with Graham Simpson and Dark Horse, mentioning that I had a picture of the latter on the drive. I also told him about the journal.

"Is it safe to speak in here?" I asked, looking around the grey boring office for any sign of a camera. I knew they had them in the interview rooms. I wasn't ruling out they had them in here too.

"It's fine," he said. "Completely confidential and private. Why?"

"Apart from you getting Simpson's journal that was with his body and running Dark Horse's photo through your database, there's something else I need."

He leaned closer. "What is it?"

"The truth. You know this suicide ruling is bullshit, right?"

His smile turned to a grimace. He stood up and locked the office door before returning to his seat. "Listen, Harley, I've got a real bad feeling about this case. I've never known the tox report or post-mortem details to come back so fast. And not only that, the chief reassigned me to another case immediately—even before we got the results back."

"So, what is this? An inside cover-up?"

He pressed his lips together for a moment, thinking. "If it is, it's coming from much higher up than this station. The chief's never acted like this before. The guy was drunk yesterday—during the day. Someone's leaning on him from above."

"How high do you think it goes?" I asked.

"Who knows? But you've got to keep a low profile on this one."

"So you'll help me, then?" I asked. "I really need that journal and Dark Horses' details."

He sighed and leaned back in his chair. He looked weary now. I could tell by the marks under his eyes he hadn't been sleeping well for a while.

"On one condition," he said.

My stomach knotted. I knew what was coming. "What?"

"You have dinner with me—just once. Tonight, at a fancy place. On me. I got a little bonus for dropping the case. I might as well use it for something good."

"And this is non-negotiable?" I said.

"I'm afraid so."

"You really are a douchebag."

"But a handsome douchebag with resources and information you need. Look, it's not like I'm asking you to go away on a dirty weekend or anything. It's just dinner. I'm lonely, Harley. I need a friend." He pouted like a baby and gave me the puppy-dog eyes.

"Fine," I said. "One lousy dinner, but that's all you're getting. I'm with Cole now." Or was I? Without talking to him, I didn't really know where we stood.

"It's a deal," Alex said, reaching out his hand.

I shook it and sat back down. "So, about what I need."

"Coming right up. I'll go to the evidence room and check if that journal is still there. I can't let you take it from the station, though."

I pulled my cell phone out of my purse. "No probs. I'll take pictures of the pages; then you can have it back."

He stood and opened the door. "Okay, give me about ten minutes. Don't go anywhere, okay?"

"Sure."

"Harley, I mean it."

I smiled a wicked smile and nodded. If he were going to annoy me, I'd at least give him something to worry about while he got the journal.

Reluctantly, he turned his back and left the office, closing the door behind him.

I waited for ten minutes. Alex hadn't got back yet, so I decided to stretch my legs. I got up and opened the door, deciding to have a look around—one never knows when one might end up in a police station and be in need of a quick exit.

The corridor had four sets of windows, two on either side. These were offices much the same as Alex's. I casually peered through each one as I wandered up the corridor.

When I came to the third one, I stopped in my tracks.

Cole was there, standing close to a redhead—a full-figured woman with breasts like airbags and lips that could suck an apple through a hosepipe. She had her hands on his shoulders as she smiled and giggled, tossing her hair back.

I stepped back so Cole wouldn't spot me out of the corner of his eye.

Every cell in my body wanted me to march in there and smack the bimbo, *then Cole*. What the hell was he doing? Was this cheap woman the reason why he hadn't called me? My face flushed with anger and hurt. I turned away and stomped back to Alex's office. I slumped in the chair and tried not to cry. I was too strong to cry, dammit!

But the tears still flowed.

How could he? We'd only just got together, after years of solid friendship.

I smashed my fist against the desk and stood up. I would give that no-good scumbag a piece of my mind. I opened the door and was about to go after Cole when I walked straight into Alex, bouncing off his firm, muscular chest.

"Easy," he said. "Going somewhere?"

We locked eyes, and he must have seen the hurt in my face. "Harley, what's happened?"

Pointing to Cole's office, I said, "My ratbag of a boyfriend is playing nicey-nicey with some cheap-ass tart, that's what."

"Come on inside before everyone hears you." Alex pushed me into the office and locked the door behind him. He forced me to sit in the chair and took his position opposite me. He handed me a box of tissues from the drawer.

"It's not what you think," Alex said.

I interrupted with a really ugly blow of my nose. "I saw it all pretty clearly."

"She's just the informant for the case he's working."

"You're just covering up for him, just like you're covering up the Simpson case."

"That's not true, Harley. I'm going out on a limb for you here. As for the journal—it's not in evidence. I checked with the officer; someone has already signed it out."

"Who?" I asked, getting control of myself and trying to focus on the case rather than Cole. I still didn't believe Alex—men like to stick together in situations like these, especially cops.

"The chief."

"Crap, so he's definitely trying to sweep this under the carpet, then."

Alex handed me more tissues. I declined. "Look, I'm sorry about Cole, but right now, I think there are bigger things to worry about. I've known the chief for decades. He's a genuinely decent guy. If he's doing stuff like this, it's because he's being blackmailed or coerced. And if someone can do that to *him*, then we're dealing with some extremely powerful people."

"This is all a mess," I said. "How can I concentrate on a case like this with Cole getting all up in some cheap tart's inflated fun bags?"

"You can start by having dinner with me," he said, his cheeks dimpling with his cheeky smile.

"It's saying something that I'd rather go out with you than deal with Cole. Especially as you're literally the last person I'd want to spend an evening with."

"That's the spirit!"

"So about Dark Horse," I said, keeping him focused

on the job at hand. If I had to suffer a dinner with detective douchebag, I at least wanted something in return now that the journal was a no-go.

"Let me check," he said, plugging in the USB drive.

"Wait, won't the server log that you used the system? They'll know you looked him up."

"You really think I'm that green?" Alex said, shaking his head. "Don't worry about it. I have a guy in IT. He's given me a secure account to use. When I was in the fraud department, I had to cross a few jurisdiction lines within the system. It was easier to bypass them than wait for permission. All records are deleted at the end of the day when the maintenance routines run."

"Good to know," I said, thinking that this would be valuable information I could use as leverage with some of my hacker associates. I'm sure they'd love that kind of access to the police's system without it being traced.

It took a few minutes for the facial recognition match to execute, but eventually it ran its course. Alex printed out a report and handed it over to me. "That's your guy."

"Leroy Herbert," I said as I stared down at a mugshot of Dark Horse. In this image, he was younger with shorter hair, but it was definitely him. He was even wearing the same pendant and chain.

"Forty-two years old, charges on three counts of fraud, deception, and assault. Sentenced to five years at Her Majesty's pleasure in a maximum security prison,"

Alex said, reading out his rap sheet. "Underwent psychological assessment and was released on parole for good behaviour after three years. While inside, he registered his own church, calling his group the Heruda."

"Interesting," I said, scanning the information. This was all starting to add up. "This guy looks like the type who would kill a defenceless old man for a book of secrets."

"A what?"

I brought Alex up to speed about the book and the whole situation with Bethany.

"I really don't think you should continue with this," he said. "This is not a nice guy. And with the way the case is being handled, this could be far too large for you—and Cordelia. I still care about her, despite our failed marriage."

"So you'll help us, then," I said it as a statement. "Because we're not stopping. Once we start a job, we finish it. So if you want us safe, I suggest you join Team Cordi as an underling and help us find Dark Horse. He's one of the best leads we've got, and we need to know where he was on the day of Simpson's murder."

"Or suicide," Alex said.

I cocked an eyebrow. "Really? You think that's still a possibility? For a detective, your instincts are as blunt as a butter knife."

"Instincts are one thing," he said, "but being reckless and jumping to conclusions is another. I take the first as a guide and use rationale and facts to build a theory."

"Screw all that. This guy's our lead. Now, check your little computer and see if you have an address for this whack job."

"One of these days, Harley, you're really going to get yourself in trouble."

I just smiled back at him as he searched the records.

After a moment he looked up. "No current address," he said. "But, there is an address of an old girlfriend he was with before he got locked up."

"Bingo! Print it off and I'll be out of your hair—for now."

"I'll see you tonight," he said. "I'll text you the details. Wear something… nice."

"I'll see if I've got a HAZMAT suit."

I grabbed the information and left Alex to get on with his job. I didn't bother to look in at Cole as I walked out of the station.

I had a horse to find.

While I was on the train, I checked my cell and found that I had a number of emails from Cordi. I was impressed she had remembered what I had showed her, but I dreaded what she had sent.

She was still new to computers and emailing. I fully expected a whole bunch of gibberish, but when I opened them, they instantly got my attention.

They were pictures of Dark Horse at some club. Each picture showed him with a group of girls all dressed in slutty goth clothes. One of the emails had a message from Cordi: *Do you recognise the girl in this one?*

I enlarged the image on the cell phone's display and slid it around until I found the girl's face. I did, in fact, recognise her. She was the punk librarian who worked in the Notting Hill Gate Library.

Cordi and I once visited there for research. This was back before I had taught her how to use a computer, and also the first time I had met Alex. I remember at the time it seemed odd for a punk to be working in a library.

I replied to Cordi's email, saying I did recognise her.

I got another email from Cordi that simply said: *I've found a few leads and... another suspect! This is huge. Be back soon!*

I was excited to find out what she had found.

***

When I got back to Cordi's place, I went inside and stopped in my tracks, gasping with surprise. There, at my feet, was a man's body lying in the hallway—and not moving.

Monty *merped* at me as he started to sniff the man's ear.

To my horror, he started to bite on it as though it were a cat toy.

"Cordi!" I shouted, not sure where in the maze of a house she was. "Your cat is eating a dead man!"

Chapter 9

Cordi's head popped out from the door on the right that led to the living room. She was smiling wide and had a mischievous glint in her eye.

I stared at her, my arm pointing to the dead man. "Cordi, dead guy in your house, being eaten by your cat. This is pretty unusual, no? What's going on? Who is he? Are you okay?"

Cordi laughed and stepped out into the hall, shooing Monty away from the dead man.

The cat just glared at her and made a burping sound as he skittered away into another room.

Bending down, Cordi grabbed the man by the shirt on his back. She lifted it up with a grunt. His arms dangled down.

I was frozen to the spot, trying to understand what on earth was going on.

"I call him Lawrence," Cordi said, shifting his body upright. His head flopped down against his chest. "I found him in the loft. I was clearing out some of Auntie's old stuff, and I found him lying there in a closet, completely naked and covered in dust."

My eyes widened as I pictured that image.

"He was dead up there? How did you get him down here? And shouldn't you call the police or something?"

Cordi grinned at me and let go of Lawrence.

His body fell forward and bounced off the floor.

"I don't think the police would be too interested in an old film prop," Cordi said.

"A prop? Cordi! I thought he was real! You scared the crap out of me for a moment. I thought you'd gone completely mental or something."

"He's great, isn't he? They used him in *Indiana Jones and the Temple of Doom* as a background extra."

"Why Lawrence?" I asked. It seemed an odd name to give a prop—although it's not like I had a lot of knowledge in what a rubber human ought to be called.

Cordi shrugged. "He kind of looks like a Lawrence."

"I'll take your word for that. Is he... anatomically correct?"

Cordi's eyes widened, and she blushed slightly. "Not quite," she said. "Poor Lawrence is a eunuch."

"Poor guy. No wonder he was hiding in the closet. What are you doing with it, anyway?"

"I have someone coming over later to collect it. I thought it would be good to start clearing out some of this old stuff. Auntie really cluttered the place up, and she doesn't want to store it herself. Come on, let me show you what I found."

I stepped over Lawrence's prone form and followed

Cordi into the kitchen.

She had the laptop on with various windows already open.

I poured us both a cup of tea and waited for Cordi to explain what she had found.

"Here," she said, double-clicking on an email. It had a scanned image of a handwritten letter. "It's a note written to Simpson thirty years ago, by Lord Buttsworth. Well, he wasn't a lord then, but it certainly shines a light on him as a potential suspect."

I scanned through the letter, trying to make out the spidery cursive text. "I can barely read it," I said. "It's like trying to read a doctor's prescription."

"Here," Cordi said, turning the laptop to face her. "I'm used to reading old documents." She bent lower and squinted at the screen, reading out Lord Buttsworth's letter.

"'My dear friend,' he starts off," Cordi said. "I have been wrestling with this issue for more than a decade and a half. I feel that after this much time you deserve to know the truth.

"I'm sure you're aware of the date, at the time of my writing this. Our mutual friend Skudder committed suicide. It's a terrible business still, even though we were just fourteen at the time. The headmaster had a breakdown shortly after that event, unable to believe that Skudder could take his life in such a manner on his watch."

I became rigid in my chair as Cordi continued on.

"Back then, I'm sure you remember how we all thought Skuds did it because of his parents' divorce. He was particularly fond of his father, Captain Skudder, I recall. It must have crushed him to discover his role model and hero was a cheat and drunkard. Well, Simpo, I'm terribly ashamed to say that it wasn't his parents' separation that drove dear old Skuds to kill himself."

"This is terrible," I said, imagining these young boys having to deal with the suicide of one of their friends.

"It gets worse," Cordi said, scanning to find her place on the letter. "You may or may not remember the crowd I fell in with after I had joined the rugger team. They were a bad lot, Simpo, rotten to the core. I was weak, you see. And once I joined the team, I was dragged into their murky world of initiations and generally awful behaviour. I was too young and too weak to stand up to them.

"Poor old Skuds, though, was weaker still and didn't have it in him to get onto the rugger team, despite numerous tryouts. Realising sports weren't his bag, he started up the chess club—and was rather successful at it, by all accounts. But to the rugger crowd, he was a let-down and a nerd, and they couldn't stand for that, especially as he was our friend."

I gripped the edge of the table, waiting to hear the revelation that was surely coming.

Cordi took a sip of tea before she continued narrating the letter.

"I'm waffling, Simpo, and I'm sure you can tell from my handwriting this isn't coming easy, but then it shouldn't. I have to live with what I did to Skuds, your best friend. I find I can't really say Skuds was my friend, because if he was, then how could I have done what I did?

"I make no excuses for my actions. I understand why I did it, but it doesn't make it right, and only by confessing to you can I put the record straight.

"Skuds, our dearest Skudder, killed himself because of *me*, Simpo. As part of the moronic crowd I had got caught up in, it was my initiation to bully poor Skuds and break him down. I had to humiliate him in front of the whole school. So I did. I'm sure you remember that day. It will forever live long in my memory, sadly.

"After I did what I did, Skuds was never the same. A week later, he took his life, unable to face the school after I had bullied him and humiliated him. I broke his spirit, and it killed him. It was all my fault.

"I, Gerald Buttsworth, am to blame for the whole sorry affair.

"I understand if you never speak with me again, Simpo. There's no forgiving what I did, or for keeping the truth to myself all these years. I just hope you can someday forgive yourself for not being there to help Skuds. I know you thought you were partly to blame for not being with him on that fateful day, but if it wasn't for my rotten actions, Skuds would still be with us today.

"I'm so sorry, so very truly sorry. Gerald."

Cordi looked up at me and said, "That's it, the letter in full. Quite the confession, eh?"

"Wow," I said. "That was intense. Schooldays are tough, but that…" I shook my head as I thought about poor Graham Simpson having lost his best friend at such a young age. No wonder he retreated into books and literature. "So this Lord Buttsworth, what do we know about him? And what was the result of this letter?"

"That's where it gets really interesting," Cordi said, turning the laptop to me. "Buttsworth wasn't a lord then, but is now. He's very high up in the scheme of things and only a few marriages outside of the royal family. He's one of the richest men in the UK with a portfolio worth over two billion pounds."

"That's quite a sizeable fund," I said.

"Indeed. The odd thing was that Simpson never got that letter when it was written. Over twenty years had passed since then. If you read the emails, it seems Simpson only found it a few weeks ago, stuck inside an old parcel that he found in his basement. When he opened it, naturally it was quite the shock. It seems that Buttsworth realised Simpson had never got the letter and kept quiet as he worked his way up through the establishment, making a huge fortune for himself. All the while, Simpson remained somewhat of a hermit, forever blaming himself for not being there for his best friend."

"So let me guess," I said. "When Simpson read the letter recently, he got back in touch with Buttsworth and told him what he thought of him."

"Something like that, yes," Cordi said.

"And given Buttsworth's exalted position these days, I'm assuming he now didn't want that truth coming out?"

"Got it in one, girl."

Cordi and I fist-bumped like cool kids and felt good about ourselves for a while as we finished our tea. "This would give Buttsworth the perfect motive to want Simpson dead," I said.

"It sure would. Especially as Simpson refused his offer of a financial bribe." Cordi pointed to the last email in the chain. "You can see that Buttsworth arranged to meet with Simpson the night before his death. Simpson only agreed to see him to get him off his back. He refused the bribe. After that... who knows what happened? He's dead, and as far as Buttsworth's concerned, he's off the hook. He obviously didn't realise that Simpson had scanned the letter and kept it on his computer."

"Do we know for certain this Skudder person exists and this isn't just some weird hoax or game?" I said.

Cordi handed me a printout. On the paper was a death certificate for one Clifford Gaynor Skudder.

"That's pretty definite," I said. "How did you get this?"

"I have my ways," Cordi said with a sly smile.

"I'm sure you do. You're quite the dark horse yourself. Talking of which, I'm assuming we're going to speak with our local punky librarian? If she could connect us with Dark Horse, we might shed some light on his dealings with Simpson."

Finishing her mug of tea, Cordi thought for a moment. "I think you're right. It's the obvious lead we have and worth following up. I'd also like to try to speak with this Buttsworth."

"I can't imagine that'll be easy," I said. "It's a lord we're talking about; I doubt we can just rock up at his house and accuse him of murder. I hear they don't handle that kind of thing well."

Cordi nodded her head, deep in thought. "I'll think of something," she said. "By the way, I spoke with the private seller Mr. Cheesebury said he visited. He's going to send you a copy of the video footage. I hope you don't mind that I gave him your email address."

"Not at all," I said. "It'll be helpful to eliminate someone from the equation, or not, as the case may be. Did he say when he'd send it?"

"In a day or two, he had some errands to run or something. Ooh, I just remembered; how did it go with

Alex? Did that ratbag give you any information?"

I sighed and slumped into my chair. I had forgotten about him for a moment, but the realisation that I had a date with him later that day pressed down on my shoulders. There's no way I could tell Cordi that.

Being his ex, I don't think she'd appreciate me dining with him.

"There's some interesting developments there," I said.

"Oh?"

"The journal is no longer in evidence. The chief of Alex's department checked it out. Alex thinks it stinks as much as we do, but is worried someone from higher up is leaning on the chief to keep it all hush-hush."

"High up, you say? Maybe a… lord?" Cordi tapped her fingers on her chin as she considered the possibility.

I had to admit, it seemed possible. The pieces were slowly beginning to show themselves, but I couldn't quite grasp at their meaning yet. We had a number of suspects and only circumstantial evidence.

"There might be something in that," I said. "But we need more information first. I got more background info on Dark Horse. Here." I pulled the printout from my pocket and handed it to Cordi.

She took the paper and read the details. "Leroy? He doesn't look like a Leroy."

"But he doesn't really look like a Dark Horse, either," I said.

"I don't know; he's got that dark bit sorted. He's quite the bad boy if his rap sheet is anything to go by. And given he met with Simpson in the morning, he's looking like the prime suspect at the moment."

"Any more leads on the diary?" I asked.

Cordi shook her head. "Not yet. I think we need to investigate Dark Horse and his band of merry Heruda whack jobs, as that's the only real connection we've got to work on."

"And we really need that journal of Simpson's," I said. "That will likely give us the breakthrough we need." I looked at the clock on the kitchen wall and realised I had better hurry up and get showered and dressed. I had that dinner date with Alex to deal with.

"What is it?" Cordi asked, looking at me intently. "You look worried about something."

"You're freaky when you do that," I said. "It's like you're a psychic. But yeah, I've got a date tonight."

Cordi's face lit up as she beamed a smile. "So you got in touch with Cole? That is exciting. Hopefully with just the two of you together, you can work out any issues."

I couldn't find it in me to tell her the truth, that I was dating her ex-husband as part of the deal for him to help me. It would only cause her undue stress, and right now I needed to keep Alex on side if we were to break this case.

"Come with me," Cordi said, standing and taking my hand. "I've got the perfect dress for you. I found it when I was cleaning out the loft earlier. It's all clean and laundered and will fit you perfectly."

I couldn't protest as Cordi dragged me like an excited schoolgirl upstairs to her room. She rifled through her closet and pulled out the dress in question. "Well?" she said. "What do you think?"

"Wow, Cordi, that's stunning!"

At least if I was going to have to put up with Alex, I would look and feel good doing it.

Chapter 10

I stepped out of the black cab and tottered across the road to the Mint Leaf. A posh West End restaurant. It was Alex's choice. We could have gone somewhere more downmarket, but it seemed he wanted to impress me.

I wish he didn't. I already felt bad about wearing Cordi's dress after she thought I was seeing Cole. Though that was entirely my fault. I could have come clean, but I chickened out, not wanting to drive a wedge between us.

Her relationship with Alex since the divorce went through had been patchy, to say the least.

I wished I had brought the *Dr. Who* scarf. I was freezing in the little body-hugging dress. It was beautiful, though. Made from deep red silky material, it had a plunging neckline that showed off a lot more flesh than I was used to.

At least it wasn't too short, coming down below the knee.

Cordi even made me borrow a pair of her heels to go with it. Although they were a size too large, they still fit reasonably well. They were the same colour as the dress.

I tottered across the road like an amateur drag queen. I wasn't used to such delicate shoes. I usually wore biker boots with flat heels, or my old battered Converse shoes.

With a clutch purse tucked under my arm and my black hair swept back, I looked classier than I had ever done.

Classy wasn't a style I had ever really gotten to grips with.

My reflection in the restaurant's window caught me off guard.

Weird. I didn't look like me anymore.

I took a deep breath and entered the restaurant. Hopefully it would be a short date and I could quickly forget about this whole arrangement and get back to the case.

The Mint Leaf was stunning inside.

With dark wooden floors and candlelit tables spread out in a sweeping snowflake shape, impeccably dressed waiters and waitresses sauntered through the place, carrying plates of food resembling works of art.

I arrived at a podium and waited, enjoying the heat on my skin. A heater above me was blowing a stream of warm air. Nice touch. I was glad that Cordi had dressed me up. For once, I didn't look out of place. If I had worn my usual outfit of jeans and T-shirt, I doubt they'd even let me in.

A maître d⊠ approached me and took my name.

"Ms. Hill. *Oui.* Follow me," he said in a thick French accent, turning on his heel and leading me through the restaurant.

We went around to the rear of the establishment. I groaned inwardly when I saw our table—probably the best table in the house. Sitting there with a wide grin, and wider eyes, Alex looked up at me. He stood and shooed the Frenchman away. He pulled my chair out and waited for me to sit.

"Harley," he said, "glad you could make it. I thought you might have stood me up."

"I still might," I replied, taking the seat and trying not to show him I was actually impressed. The table was by a window overlooking a pond lit up with a series of discreet solar lamps in the long grass.

A candle flickered in the middle of the table. Alex had already ordered drinks. A bottle of champagne nestled inside a chilled bucket. Two glasses were poured.

Still grinning like a cat that got the tuna, Alex sat down opposite and stared at me. "Nice dress," he said.

The desire to reach for an invisible shawl to wrap around me came quickly. "Stop looking at me like that," I said. "You're making me feel uncomfortable."

"Did Cordi give you the dress?" he asked. There was a hint of slyness to his eyes that I didn't like.

"Yes," I said. "Why?"

"I just recognise it, that's all."

"*Ew*, you're not fantasising, are you? That's gross." I suddenly felt entirely icky wearing the dress now. All thoughts of being classy were now overridden with the thought of Alex remembering…

"Kinda," he said. "It's difficult not to when you're wearing the dress I married her in."

"What? This is Cordi's wedding dress?"

Alex nodded, amusement spread all over his annoying face.

"That's…" I burned with embarrassment and horror, picturing him unzipping it from Cordi. "Why didn't she say anything?"

"You didn't tell her you were here with me tonight, that's why," he said.

"How do you know? You planted a bug on me or something?"

"No. Simple deduction, Sherlock. If you had told her you were here with me tonight, there's no way Cordi would have given you that dress."

"Aren't you the sharp one," I said before swallowing half the glass of champagne.

It was a good one; I'd give him that. I filled it up, determined that if I was going to have to suffer his overbearing charm for the evening, I'd do it with the help of alcohol. He would be paying, so I wanted to make sure it hurt him in the wallet so he couldn't bribe me again.

He'd learn I wasn't a cheap date.

"Seriously, stop staring at my chest," I said.

"You're the one with the puppies on parade."

I picked up the menu and unfolded it to block his view of me.

He just laughed in that self-satisfied way of his.

An older gentleman with grey hair at the table next to us was looking over at me while his wife was chatting about something and gesticulating wildly with her fork. His face looked like how I felt, both of us clearly wishing we were somewhere else.

Hang in there, man. It'll soon be over, I wanted to say to my fellow-suffering comrade. I gave him a sympathetic smile instead and returned my attentions to the menu.

I made sure I picked the smallest, and most expensive, meal. Mostly to hit Alex in the wallet, but also so I could get to the dessert without filling myself up. I ordered a chocolate fudge layer cake that was almost as expensive as the main.

Despite the company, I was thoroughly enjoying the dessert—right up until the moment I heard a familiar voice from behind me. Cole Lockland, my supposed boyfriend.

His words froze me in place. I couldn't look around.

"It's him, isn't it?" I whispered to Alex as I leaned across the table.

"Sure is," he said. "That's kind of awkward, no?"

"You're enjoying this far too much," I said. "I don't

like the way you delight in my awkwardness." Which was ironic seeing as how I caught him in a compromising situation just a few a months ago.

While Cordi and I were on another case, we had to interview a dominatrix in a home/dungeon workplace. Inside, she was seeing a masked client. Turns out it was Alex. He had a spanking fetish. Cordi hadn't known. From the car, I had seen Alex leave the building.

"Consider this payback," he said with a smile that made his cheeks dimple.

To be fair, I did use the whole spanking thing against him a couple of times, but then he'd been a complete ass to Cordi and me, so all was fair, right? Just because he was handsome and charming didn't mean he could get his own way all the time.

"He's two tables behind you," Alex said. "And has company."

I really didn't want to look round, but it was like those horror films with the stupid college girl standing outside the basement door. She knows there's something down there. *You* know there's something down there. It's a sure death, but the girl still opens the door and goes down there to get killed by the psycho/monster/ghost/evil cat.

But just like that horror movie college girl, I turned my head—and kind of wished I didn't.

There was Cole… *my* Cole, looking hot as ever in his beautifully tailored black suit and tie, getting cosy with the bimbo from the station.

Now I thought I was wearing a tight, revealing dress, but this so-called informant was wearing something that looked like it was sprayed on, showing off her every surgeon-enhanced curve and bulge.

I watched with increasing dread as she and Cole flirted, held hands, and looked into each other's eyes across the candlelight. When she kissed him, I spun round and stuffed my face with the remaining chocolate layer cake. It filled my cheeks, making me look like a hamster stuffing my pouches for winter.

But I didn't care.

It was either that or ugly crying.

My hands shook as I scooped the fork into the last of the cake. My vision was blurry with tears, but I refused to let Cole get to me. I focused on the job at hand.

After I had swallowed my cake, I slouched in my chair. I was stuffed. I didn't care if it looked like I was five months pregnant with a cake baby. I was already humiliated.

And I no longer cared about Cole's brazen behaviour. Which, of course, was a massive lie, but I guess I just couldn't handle it. I had to carry on, pretend all was fine and I hadn't seen anything.

"So," I said to Alex. "Who's doing the cover-up? Who's above your chief who would have a stake in this?"

"Let's not talk about shop," Alex said, reaching for

the champagne bottle.

I slapped his wrist away. "It's that or I go right now," I said.

He shrugged and leaned back in his chair as a waitress cleared our table. When she left, he moved forward and lowered his voice.

"Okay, fine. After you left yesterday, I overheard the chief talking to some posh guy from the House of Lords—he was in the station doing a walkabout, supposedly seeing how things were being run. The government are doing an audit into police methods, apparently."

"Wait, a lord? Buttsworth by any chance?"

"Yeah, that's the guy. Real old and stuffy. Proper upper-class type. Part of the old boys' network. He and the chief go back to school days, by all accounts."

"Holy crap! Dude, this is it, this is the break in the case, surely!" I quickly filled him in about Buttsworth's letter to Simpson and their meeting arranged for the day before the latter's death.

Alex's face became serious and he tapped his fingers on the table as he thought. "It must be him that has the journal, then," he said. "Perhaps Simpson had the letter with it?"

"There's far too many connections here to overlook this guy," I said. "How do we get to him? We really need to have a chat."

"You can't just go accusing a member of the House

of Lords of murder," Alex said.

"Who said anything about accuse? We can just ask him."

"No," Alex said. "You don't understand; these guys are powerful. They make bigger crimes than this go away all the time. We need to be smarter about this."

"We? You believe me now, then, that Simpson's death wasn't suicide?" I said.

"I didn't say that—it could still be suicide for all we know, but there's still threads that need looking into. Follow the evidence. That's what we do."

"You keep saying 'we'," I said. "This is mine and Cordi's investigation."

"You need me."

"Like a hole in the head."

"Now, now, sweetie, play nice."

"I'm tired of being nice," I said. "It gets me into situations like this. Listen, you've had your dinner date. I'm going to freshen up and then call a cab. If you want to help with the case, then do it, but I'm not going to be blackmailed into more dates in return for your help. Cordi and I will do it ourselves."

With that I got up and headed for the restrooms.

I walked through a door that led into a hallway. The men's and women's restrooms were opposite each other. I walked down the corridor thinking about what to say to Alex once I got back to the table when I bumped face-first into a hard, toned body.

A body I knew well.
Cole's.
Crap!

Chapter 11

I didn't have time to turn around and run.

Cole's strong hands were on my shoulders, pinning me in place. He looked down at me with those beautiful eyes of his, and despite my anger toward him, my body warmed and reacted to his gaze and touch.

"Harley, come with me," he said, looking around frantically before pushing me into the women's restroom.

"What are you doing?" I asked with a fierce growl in my voice.

Cole walked down the length of the restroom, checking into each cubicle. He returned and locked the door before turning back to me with an urgent expression on his face.

"Cole, this is crazy. What the hell are you doing?"

"We don't have much time," he said hurriedly, grabbing me close to him again.

I squirmed out of his grip. "Don't touch me," I said. "I don't know where those hands have been—though I can give it a bloody good guess, what with the living Barbie doll out there with her bits all up in your face."

"About that," he said. "It's not what you think."

"So I didn't see you kissing her? I didn't see her tongue playing hockey with your tonsils? I saw the way you looked at her, the way you touched her. Don't take me for a fool, Cole, unless you want to join Lawrence and form a comedy eunuch duo."

"Who's Lawrence?"

"A long story, just get out of my way and let me go. I don't want to speak to you right now, or perhaps ever."

"No, Harley, you'll listen to me, dammit. There's some serious crap going down."

"Yeah? Well, I have my own problems to deal with."

"Like Alex?" he said.

"Oh no," I said. "You don't get to be hurt. I'm only here because he blackmailed me. I needed a favour from him for a case, and if you want to compare situations, you'll notice my hands are nowhere near his genitalia. I can't say the same for you and Barbie."

Cole ran his hand through his hair and turned away with a sigh.

"It's a case," he said. "A big damned case that I'm up to my neck in. I can't explain everything now. Please, just trust me on this one. If you watch the news tomorrow morning, I'm sure they'll be covering it. I can tell you more then. I know how it looks."

"It looks bad, Cole, real bad."

"I know, babe, I like it about as much as you do. Here, take this; I'll call you on it tomorrow. It'll all make sense then, I promise."

He handed me a Blackberry cell phone.

"Why this?" I asked.

"I can't trust talking with you on a regular line. Not until I know this is over. This is secure."

"What's going on? You're scaring me."

"I've got to go. Barbie will wonder where I am. I can't raise any suspicions—there's people watching me. This is huge, babe, really. I have to play my part in this."

"Is it to do with Lord Buttsworth?" I asked, placing the cell phone into my clutch purse.

Cole's expression became hard and serious. "Just stay out of this, Harley. Please. And be careful what you say to Alex. Don't trust anyone."

"Not even you?" I asked.

"Tomorrow. Do as I tell you, and you'll see it all make sense, I promise with all my heart. I'd never do anything to hurt you. You know this. I've always looked out for you, and now I'm doing it again by keeping you out of this."

He leaned down and kissed me with a frantic, passionate energy that made my body melt into him. Before I could get my breath back, he unlocked the door and left me standing there, my head dizzy with his kiss—and his revelations.

I looked to the door leading back into the restaurant and then at the window at the rear of the restroom. Without any hesitation I rushed to the window, opened it, and squeezed myself through.

Alex would just have to finish the champagne himself. I landed with a bump. Luckily it was just grass, but I hit my knee, making me wince. Walking on my tiptoes, I stalked around the rear of the restaurant, going the opposite way to where Alex was sitting; otherwise he'd surely see me skulking past the pond and the lights.

A chef leaned against an open door. He stubbed out a cigarette on the gravel and went back inside. Once the door was closed, I hurried by and made my way through an alleyway until I came out at the main road.

I managed to find a black cab and got in, giving him the address to Cordi's place. I ignored his incessant talk about football and politics as I inspected the Blackberry Cole had given to me.

It was no ordinary cell phone.

The back had clearly been removed, given the scratches and marks on it. A small square plastic device poked out from the bottom. When I switched it on, there wasn't the usual Blackberry branding, just a series of symbols and letters.

Remembering what Cole said, I switched it off and hoped that tomorrow would bring some answers after all.

My mind was swirling with a hundred ideas and theories. Buttsworth seemed to be in the middle of all this; then there was Dark Horse Leroy—what role, if any, did he play?

When the cab stopped at the end of Cordi's road, I paid him and didn't wait for change. I just wanted to get inside and take a long shower.

The cab drove off and I turned around to walk the two hundred yards to Cordi's house. I got just a few feet when the heel of my right shoe caught in a loose slab of the pavement, sending me pitching forward right into a muddy puddle.

Filthy water dripped from my face and body as I staggered to my feet.

My knees were skinned and grazed. They were now probably home to a whole colony of weird and wonderful bacteria. *Wonderful!*

A perfect end to a rotten evening.

I ignored the people across the road laughing at my misfortune, picked up my clutch purse, and waddled lopsidedly on the broken shoe to Cordi's with what little dignity I had left.

The dress was a real mess. Thankfully I hadn't torn it, but I still felt terrible.

When I unlocked the door and stepped inside, I paused, fully expecting another Lawrence waiting to surprise me.

To somewhat of an anticlimax, there was just a note, from Cordi, propped up on a side table in the hall.

"Harley," it started. "Gone sleuthing with Auntie. She has a lead on the diary. Hope your evening with

Cole went well. Don't wait up, and don't be alarmed if you hear movement in the house in the early hours. That'll be me. Hopefully. I've fed Monty, so he shouldn't bother you for the rest of the night. See you in the morning. C x"

I breathed out a long sigh of relief and leaned against the table. Dirty water dripped from the dress and my hair, and I'm not ashamed to admit that I cried, just a little.

Okay, more than a little.

But can you blame me? Things were messed up, and I had just ruined Cordi's wedding dress. To make matters worse, Monty had left a stinky little gift in the hallway. Cordi had fed him okay—he just got rid of it rather quickly.

"Monty! You filthy little beast. When I get my hands on you!"

Merp.

I spun round to see Monty sitting behind me, his tail swishing back and forth across the hallway floor. His ears twitched and he blinked his one eye.

"Thanks, buddy," I said. "Like my night isn't bad enough that I have to clean up your mess. You do have a litter box, you know."

Meow. Swish.

I cleaned up his deposit like any dutiful human, slaves to cats that we are, and got changed out of Cordi's dress. I would take it to the dry cleaners tomorrow.

Hopefully they'd make it as good as new again.

I changed into my favourite PJs and slumped into the sofa of the living room. It looked much better these days. When I had first come here, the place was rammed with furniture, bookcases, and endless boxes of various detritus.

The room couldn't be described as sparse yet, but it was certainly an improvement. There was no longer a threat of being buried under a falling bookcase, and the TV was actually visible.

My eyelids began to droop. I didn't have the energy to climb the stairs, so I just lay on the sofa and hoped everything would be better in the morning.

As I was drifting off I was vaguely aware of a large, grey furry form snuggle in next to me. Monty's purr helped to send me off to sleep.

Perhaps he wasn't so bad.

He was certainly higher on the 'like' scale than either Cole or Alex right now.

I dreaded to find out what I would hear tomorrow morning when Cole called me on the suspicious Black-berry.

A thousand worrying thoughts flooded my dreams.

Nothing could prepare me for the truth of what he was involved in.

Chapter 12

Day 4

I woke to the sound of my cell phone bleeping with an email notification.

With bleary eyes, I opened my mail app to see that I had been sent a video file from Mr. Cheesebury's alibi. I then noticed the deliciously bitter scent of fresh coffee.

Like a scene from a cartoon, I got up from the sofa and followed the coffee smell into the kitchen, which was quickly becoming the unofficial hub of our operations.

We actually had a dedicated office up on the second floor, in the spare bedroom, but I suppose because the kitchen had coffee-making facilities, and cakes in the cupboards, we defaulted to there.

The clock on the wall said it was just past seven a.m. I'm hardly ever up this early.

Cordi was bent over the sink, her shoulders hunched as she scrubbed at something.

"Morning," she said cheerfully. "It looks like you had quite a rough night last night. Want to talk about it?"

When she turned to face me, I saw that her eyes were puffy. She had been crying. It was then I saw her wedding dress covered in soapsuds within the sink.

"Oh, I'm so sorry, Cordi, I really am. I didn't mean for anything to happen to your dress. Please don't cry. I promise I'll get it clean. I'll take it to the dry cleaners right away."

Cordi dried her hands on a towel and wiped her tears away.

"You sweet girl, it's fine. I'm not upset at you. I'm just..." She shrugged and dropped the wedding dress back into the sink. "Thinking of old times, I guess. I should have thrown this dress out with the rest of the stuff from the marriage. What happened to you?"

I told her about the whole night, and even admitted that it was Alex I had had the date with. She came over and hugged me. "You didn't have to keep that to yourself, Harley, dear. We're friends, I would have understood. I was married to that douchebag, so I know all about his manipulation. Us women have to stick together."

"Thanks, Cordi, you're a good friend. I just didn't want to burden you with anything. This case is really getting quite tricky, and from what I can gather from Cole and Alex, it goes way deeper than we first realised."

"About that," she said. "I've got something to tell you. Auntie and I had a bit of a breakthrough last night."

"Ah, before you do, I got Cheesebury's alibi video. Do you want to watch it?"

"Sure."

I opened the email, and we both watched the video on my cell phone. As Mr. Cheesebury had said, it showed him arriving in his car and going into the house after being greeted at the door by the private seller. Some time passed, and he was shown leaving, carrying a box of books, which he placed into the back of the car. Then he drove off. Nothing else happened, and it didn't look as though anything was wrong, though there was something about it I couldn't put my finger on. I just had a feeling that something wasn't right, but then that might have just been the anxiety I was still feeling from the night before.

"I guess Charles Cheesebury checks out," Cordi said.

"Looks like it. Well, I suppose we can focus on other leads. What was it that you wanted to talk about?"

Cordi poured a couple of cups of coffee, and I nibbled on toast as Cordi explained what she had found. "Auntie has her ways with sniffing out information. The grapevine in this case was an old friend of hers called Doris. She owns a tearoom in the West End. Doris runs a book club meeting there every week."

"So that's where you were last night?" I asked.

"You got it. It was an interesting night. The book was horrible, though, but after all the book chat, the gossip started to come out, instigated, of course, by Auntie. If there's one thing she can do well, it's drag information out of people as though they were fully willing. It's only after they've spluttered out their secrets they realise what she's done."

I chuckled at the thought of Maggie interrogating people with the promise of cake and pastries. "Okay," I said. "I'm intrigued. What did you find out?"

"The sister of the woman there works in the British Library. In the last two days, she's had three requests from different people to see a particular old pamphlet."

I placed the mug of coffee down and swallowed the final piece of buttery toast. "Let me guess," I said. "This pamphlet has something to do with the Doomsday Diary?"

"Oh indeed. But even better. It's apparently a copy of some of the pages from the diary, penned by John Dee himself. And it gets better still. Through Auntie's superior bribery skills, she has us an exclusive meeting with the curator at the British Library. We'll be the first members of the general public to see this pamphlet."

"That's fantastic. That'll definitely give us an edge over the competition. Which I'm assuming at the moment is Buttsworth and Dark Horse."

"We can't rule out other parties either. I'm still not sure about Cheesebury. Or Bethany."

"It definitely feels like an open race at the moment," I said. "Hopefully, thanks to Maggie, we'll have a head start. When's the appointment with the curator?"

"Tomorrow at four p.m. Auntie will be coming with us. I've never seen her so excited. She loves old books, so this is right up her street."

"It feels good to make some progress on this case," I said. Especially as my head was still swirling after last night. And then I remembered what Cole said. *The news!*

I rushed into the living room and switched on the TV. I waited for ten minutes until it started. Cordi joined me on the sofa. "So you think there's something to all this business with Cole, then?"

"I don't know," I said. "For years I thought he was a fence, but then it turned out he was an undercover cop for all that time. And now this cloak-and-dagger stuff with the Barbie informant... I just can't decide yet what's the truth. But I've got to at least give him an opportunity."

I sat cross-legged, biting my nails all throughout the news broadcast until the final story came up. The female news anchor shuffled her papers and looked back at the camera, announcing they had breaking news.

Every muscle in my body tensed as I watched the screen like a cat watches a mouse.

My heart nearly leapt out of my chest when a mugshot of Barbie came on screen. It then went to live footage.

"That's Cole," Cordi said, pointing at the screen.

"Yeah," I said automatically, glued to the action.

There was a bustle of paparazzi surrounding Barbie. She was pushing out her chest, like she needed any help in that department. But then as the interviewer thrust a microphone in her face, I realised that her chest was like that because her hands were cuffed behind her back, and Cole was holding onto her, leading her through the crowd and into a police car.

The camera zoomed into the car window.

Sitting next to Barbie, in the rear, was an older man in a white shirt. He was also cuffed. Panning back to Cole, the interviewer asked, "So, Detective Jonas, how does it feel to be the one who busted Gianni Lucarelli and his daughter? It's quite a coup, is it not? I'm led to understand that Mr. Lucarelli has been wanted for a decade for his role in organised crime activity."

"Sorry," Cole said. "No comment." He pushed his way through the crowd and got into a separate unmarked car that followed the police car as it drove away.

"Wow," I said. "Lucarelli is huge."

"You know him?" Cordi asked.

"Kinda, by reputation more than anything else. In my old days, before I found Cole and went straight-ish, I had done a few jobs for some people who worked for Lucarelli. The rumour was that he was a Mafia don. But then every two-bit criminal with an Italian name thinks that. I guess the rumours were true for Lucarelli after all."

"Jonas is Cole's real name?" Cordi asked.

"It's actually the other way around. Cole Lockland is his real name. As a cop, he uses Steve Jonas. But oh… crap, I just realised something."

"What is it?"

"If he's on TV, his cover is blown. Most of the London underworld knows him as Cole Lockland the fence… if it comes out that he's been undercover all this time, then they'll…" I broke off and went through my clutch purse to get the Blackberry he'd given to me.

"Oh," Cordi said, "it gets worse."

I looked up and saw a large man in a grey suit standing next to a uniformed man. The titles on the screen indicated that they were Lord Buttsworth and Chief Goodridge, Alex's superior.

I had a sinking feeling as I watched Buttsworth talk to the interviewer.

Buttsworth made me ill just looking at him. He oozed with a slimy personality that only comes from decades of privilege. His hair was clearly dyed black. His temples were silver-grey, giving him the look of a badger.

He had a wispy moustache, waxed at the ends, like Salvador Dali.

Goodridge cut an opposing figure. He was narrow shouldered and had small dark eyes hidden behind large metal-framed spectacles. His collar and tie were tight against his many chins.

"Lord Buttsworth, as judge for the Lucarelli case in the '80s, you must be pleased to see that he's been brought to justice once more for a new trial," said the interviewer as cameras all around the lord and the chief flashed and snapped away.

"Mr. Lucarelli has been at large for the past decade," Buttsworth said. "With the fine work of Chief Goodridge and his staff, we can start new proceedings."

"And will you be the judge this time?"

"That's yet to be determined. I'm sure the press will be informed on that soon. For now, if you don't mind, there's a lot of work that needs to be done." With that, Buttsworth smiled briefly at the camera and headed off toward a black Jaguar waiting at the curbside for him.

The interviewer turned to Chief Goodridge and effectively asked the same questions. I zoned out then, trying to put all the pieces together. It seemed Buttsworth was everywhere we turned.

"With him involved with this new Lucarelli case," I said. "It's going to make it much harder for us to get to him and question him about Simpson."

"It is…" Cordi said. "Unless…"

"Unless what? I don't like that look in your eye. What are you thinking?"

Cordi turned to me and with a steely gaze said, "We'll blackmail him with the letter."

My mouth dropped open at the suggestion. I didn't get a chance to say how crazy that was when the Blackberry started to chirp. I quickly answered it.

"Cole? Is that you?" I asked, my stomach tightening as I waited for the response.

"Harley, it's me. Did you see the news?"

"I did. What's going on? They just blew your cover."

"Yeah, I know, that was always going to happen. It was the only way we could get the heat off Lucarelli and me."

"What heat? I don't understand. You're scaring me, Cole. What's happening?"

"Lucarelli is innocent. I'm taking him out of the country."

"What? Why?" My hand started to shake with fear. I couldn't lose Cole now. Not when things were getting so complicated.

"I don't have much time. I have to go. You have to get rid of the cell I gave you; they'll soon find it. I'll be back in a week if everything goes well."

"Cole, please just tell me where you're going and what's going on. I can't be left in the dark; I'll go mad with worry." There was a silence that seemed to stretch on forever.

"Sicily," he said. "We're infiltrating the Mafia. They think we're doing a deal to exchange Lucarelli and me for some guys the Mafia kidnapped. It's what I've been working on all this time. I couldn't say anything because I wanted you out of it."

"But why blow your cover? It doesn't make sense."

"I can't explain fully, there isn't time, but it'll flush out a number of gangsters involved with this operation. As I speak, there's a number of them coming after me—but there's people waiting for them."

"Crap, Cole, the police are using you as bait! What happens when you come back?"

Silence.

"Wait, you are coming back, right?"

"That's the plan. Just stay out of trouble—and stay away from Buttsworth. Okay, they're here. I've got to go, babe. I love you."

I love you too, I wanted to say, but the line was already dead. How could he wait for that moment to finally tell me he loves me?

What if he didn't come back? I felt sick.

"What's happening?" Cordi asked. I told her everything, and we both sat there in silence, contemplating Cole's likely fate. I almost wished he didn't tell me. Although I knew he was incredibly capable and smart, working with guys like Lucarelli and the Mafia wasn't something that could ever go smoothly.

"I need to do something," I said, standing up. "I can't sit around brooding for Cole, I'll go bonkers. I know he would want me to continue working—even if he did warn us to stay away from Buttsworth."

"But you're not going to listen to him, are you?"

"Hell no. Buttsworth's guilty; I feel it in my bones. We're going to nail that guy. In the meantime, let's go talk with our punk-librarian friend. We need Dark Horse's current address. I want to make some real headway in this case."

"Let's do it," Cordi said.

I took the blackberry out to the backyard and fetched a hammer from Cordi's small, ramshackle tool shed. With three heavy whacks, I smashed the phone to pieces and threw the remains into the trash along with Monty's cat litter. I hated doing it, losing the one connection to Cole I had, but I needed to trust him and do as he had said—even if I did ignore his warning about Buttsworth.

Hey, I couldn't let him have it all his own way, and I'd still give him a piece of my mind when he came back. You didn't tell someone you love them before going undercover into the Mafia.

Unless he didn't think he would get another chance...

I couldn't keep thinking like that. I needed to focus on shaking the librarian down for information on Dark Horse.

Chapter 13

Cordi and I arrived at the Notting Hill Gate Library shortly after noon.

The place was almost deserted. There was just a single older lady hovering around at the back, sorting through a table of old books for sale—old titles that were being replaced. On another day, I'd have been there with her, searching for bargains, but we were there on business.

Cordi and I approached the front desk.

A woman, probably in her sixties, with beige skin, beige hair, and a beige cardigan smiled gently at us. "How can I help," she said, whispering, even though there was only one other person here.

"We're looking for someone who works here. A woman with short dark hair... kind of punk-ish?"

"Oh, you must mean Jessica."

I shrugged. "Sorry, I didn't get her name, but it's important we speak with her. Is she in today?"

"She just popped out... oh, wait, here she comes now."

I turned to follow the librarian's gaze.

Jessica walked through the double doors carrying a

white cardboard box. She looked up at us, her eyes shadowed with deep black kohl. She wore her hair longer than the last time we had seen her. She had it curled, and it bounced on her shoulders with each step of her heavy boots—the same kind of boots I was wearing.

She wore a short tartan skirt over black leggings. I liked her style.

It seemed we shopped in the same places.

"Jessica, dear, these ladies have come to see you," Ms. Beige said.

Jessica gave us a leery look before placing the box on the counter. She opened the lid. "Donut, Marge?"

"Oh, thank you, dear, but I'm watching my figure... but... oh, you know what, you only live once, right?" Marge took a donut from the box.

Jessica turned to us and raised a pencilled eyebrow. She rested her arm on hip, all full of attitude. She cut such a conflicting image to Marge that I almost wanted to laugh.

"Well?" Jessica said. "You wanted to speak with me? What's this about?"

"Is there somewhere private we could go?" I asked.

Marge's eyes widened as she looked at me, then Jessica. I dreaded to think what was going through her mind.

"Depends," Jessica said. "If it's about the grimoire, I'm afraid it's already booked out for the next three months."

"Grimoire?" Cordi asked.

"The spell book," Jessica said. "Since we got it in, we've been inundated by witches, stupid kids, really, wanting to get their grubby little mitts on it."

"We're not witches," I said defensively. "And no, we're not here for some grimoire. We're here about a... *horse*."

Her eyes narrowed. She closed the donut box and walked past us. "Follow me."

Cordi smiled and nudged me gently in the arm. "Good work," she whispered as we followed Jessica through a door marked 'staff'.

As soon as we got inside the compact room, Jessica dropped the box of donuts onto a white table covered in coffee stains. A whiteboard hung on the wall above it with various Post-it notes attached. Motivational phrases were written in red pen. One said, "Smile on the inside, and you'll smile on the outside."

Jessica was neither smiling on the inside nor the outside.

"What the hell is this about?" she snapped, looking me up and down with a sneer as though she were sizing me up for a fight.

"We just want to ask you a few questions," Cordi said with a soft voice, trying to calm her down. The girl looked tense and ready to lash out at any minute.

"I'm not with him, or *them*, anymore. I've told the police that so many times I'm fed up with it. When will you people leave me alone? I had nothing to do with his crimes then, and nothing to do with him now."

"Are you talking about Leroy Herbert," I said. "Aka Dark Horse?"

"Of course, who do you think, Santa Claus? Just what the hell are you here for?"

"Look, we're not here about any past crimes. We just want to know where we can find Leroy."

"Who are you people?" she said, squinting at us.

Cordi handed Jessica one of our new business cards. She took it with her black-nail-polished fingers and read the card aloud. "Silvers & Hill Finders Agency? What's that all about?"

"We find stuff," I said. "We're looking for something, and we believe Leroy can help us with that. His name has come up in our investigations, and that led us to you. All we want is an address and a little info."

She seemed to be coming around, preferring my straight talking. She sat down at the table and indicated for us to take a seat, which we did.

"Donut?" she asked.

"Sure," I said, taking one. It was made with strawberry jam. My favourite.

"So what's he done now?" Jessica asked.

"Nothing as far as we know," Cordi said. "We've been hired to find a particular item for a client of ours. We know they were in contact with Leroy. We were hoping to talk with him to see if he could help us find this item."

Jessica took a massive bite of her donut, getting sugar all round her dark purple lips. "What's the item," she said as she chewed.

"Just some old book," I said, waving my hand as though it wasn't important.

She nodded her head as she continued to chew. After she swallowed the donut, she looked at me and said, "This is not some weird sex thing, is it? You're not one of his cult groupies?"

"Cult?" I asked. "I don't know anything about that. I've never met him before. I only knew of his connection to you because I found a photo on Facebook of you and him at some club."

"*His* club," she said. "The Black Fang. It's where he runs his cult."

"What's the name of the cult?" Cordi asked.

I already had a good idea, but I wanted Jessica to confirm it.

"The Heruda, it's some stupid old thing he got from a book. They're all a little cracked over there, in the head, you know what I mean? They're all into that black magic crap. They think they can actually do stuff. To be honest, as far as Leroy is concerned, it's just an excuse for weird sex and orgies. That's one of the reasons I broke it off with him years back."

"You were his girlfriend?" I asked.

She nodded.

Her address must have been the one listed on his rap sheet.

"Thanks for helping us out," I said. "We really appreciate it. We won't take up much more of your time."

She shrugged, seemingly bored now. "S'okay, I'm on my lunch break, and it's not exactly busy around here these days. Which is a real shame. If people read more often, our society wouldn't be so stupid, right?"

"I guess so," I said. "So, do you know his home address?"

"The fool lives at his club. He can't afford his own place, so he just stays there. Sleeps through the day, and runs the club at night. It's easy to find. Just Google *'Black Fang Club'*. He's got a cheesy website with all the details on it. But if I were you, I'd have nothing to do with him."

"Why's that?" I asked

"He's bad, you know, inside. Not a good cookie at all. I fell for his charisma once, but soon learned he was basically a psychopath. He'd like you, though," she said, pointing to me. "Young, and with the right look."

"What do you mean?" I asked.

"You dress like you're a bad girl, but you're a good girl on the inside. He likes that hidden innocence. Gets off on the idea that he can corrupt people with his will. Like I said, he's a few choc chips short of a cookie."

"We could use that," Cordi said. "To our advantage."

"Oh dear, what do you have in mind?" I wasn't looking forward to what Cordi was thinking. She had the mischievous look in her eye again.

"We go to the club and get you in front of Leroy, and then you use your charms to find out what we need to know."

"You won't get in," Jessica said, wiping the sugar from her lips. "Members only and he picks the members. He's a control freak like that. He mostly does it so he can keep the ratio of women to men much higher. Less competition for him that way."

"Classy guy," I said. "And I don't really like the idea of being bait for a madman."

"What is it that you think he's got?" Jessica asked, trying to be casual about it. I could see the interest in her face, though.

"We can't really say," Cordi said. "Client confidentiality."

"That's a shame," Jessica said. "I was going to offer to help you get in. But if you can't trust me, then... well, you two are on your own. Good luck with that."

She stood up and made to leave the room. I shared a glance with Cordi. We had an opportunity here, and I didn't want to blow it. This was the best lead we had on the case, and it would really help us if we had someone with first-hand knowledge of Leroy and the Heruda on our side.

Cordi nodded, clearly understanding my unspoken request.

"Wait, Jessica, listen, if we tell you what it is we're looking for, would you help us get into the club and meet Leroy? That's all you need to do; we'll take it from there."

She turned and leaned against the door, putting her hands on her hips.

"You're getting far more out of the bargain than me," she said.

"What do you want? Surely we can work something out and help each other."

She thought about it for a moment.

"We might be able to come to an arrangement now that I think about it. But how do I know I can trust you two?"

"We could ask the same thing," Cordi said.

"Hmm, fair point. So we have mutual mistrust. That's as good as anything, I suppose. Okay, here's what I suggest. When I was with him, he took something of mine, and I want it back. It'll be in the club, probably the safe in his office. That's where he keeps trophies of his conquests. You tell me what it is you're trying to find for your client and retrieve my goods and I'll get you into the club and introduce you to Leroy."

Safe-cracking. Interesting. I had done it once or twice before, so I wasn't a complete novice at it, but I was no expert, especially if I didn't know the make and model of safe. But then I knew, through Cole, certain people who could probably help me out with that.

"What do you think?" I said to Cordi.

She took a breath and exhaled. "It's up to you, Harley. I'm game for it if you are. It's as good a break in the case we've got."

"Okay, Jessica, we'll do it. What is it he has of yours?"

"A silver bracelet. It's not especially valuable in monetary terms, but it was a gift from my grandma. I loved her so much, and it broke me when that swine stole it. It's the only thing of hers I had left—everything else perished in a house fire."

"I totally understand," I said. And I could. Both of my parents were dead, and I had nothing of theirs. I could relate to Jessica wanting something tangible of her grandma's to link them together across generations.

"So what is it you two are after?" she asked.

"A book," Cordi said. "A special book. Well, a diary to be exact."

The cogs seemed to whir in Jessica's mind as she put two and two together. Then her mouth dropped open as the realisation dawned on her. "Oh my god, you think Leroy has the Doomsday Diary, don't you?"

I didn't know whether her knowing that was a good sign or a bad one. I guessed I had to wait and see. For now, it looked like we our own little punk ally.

Chapter 14

Cordelia packed her Mercedes at the end of my brother's road.

I really didn't want to go back.

We sat there for five minutes in silence.

Eventually Cordi spoke. "It's better to get it over with," she said. "You'll never know what he'll say otherwise. All these years you've wondered what happened to your brother and sisters; this is your chance. You've got to take it."

"What if he doesn't want to know?" I asked. "With this whole thing with Cole going on, I'm not sure I could handle it."

Cordi took my hand into hers. "I know it's difficult. And I won't force you. If you want us to leave, I'll turn the car around and we can head back home."

I closed my eyes and tried to clear my head and think straight, but it was a whirlwind of mixed emotions and fears. It was true that I had wondered my entire life where my brother and sisters were, but now that I was here, just a few hundred feet away, the reality felt like a lead weight in my legs, pinning me in place.

"It's not really the rejection I'm worried about," I said. "It's the opposite. What if he accepts me? What then? I've not known any of my family for my entire life; that's a lot of catching up to do. A lot of emotion. I don't know anything about these people. What if their lives are full of tragedy? How would I cope with all that new information? Would I even still be me after knowing all that?"

"I'm afraid I can't answer that," Cordi said. "I know it's tough and scary, but you have to make that decision."

"What would you do?" I asked.

"I'd probably hide in a cupboard until it all went away," Cordi said. "I'm a coward like that. But you're not, Harley. Since I've known you, one thing I've learned is that you're incredibly strong. Stronger than you probably realise."

"Urgh, Cordi, you're not making this easy," I said, chuckling away my anxiety.

"I'm sorry. I'll come to the door with you, if that would help."

"You're talking like I've already made up my mind to go," I said.

"I think you have, haven't you?"

I guessed she was right. The fact I hadn't asked Cordi to turn around and go home immediately told me everything I needed to know: I had already decided I would do this; I was just now trying to build up the courage to see him—again.

With luck, this time I wouldn't make such an arse of myself and require rescuing.

"Okay," I said. "I'm going. I'll do it on my own. Will you wait for me, though? Just in case I need to make a quick getaway. I'll call you if I'm staying longer—I can catch a train back before we have to go to the club with Jessica tonight."

"Don't worry. I'll wait right here for you. I have the entire collection of Johnny Cash on CD, so take as long as you need."

"Right then, I guess I'm finally doing this. Wish me luck!"

"Good luck," Cordi said, squeezing my shoulder for encouragement.

I took a deep breath and got out of the car. I closed the door and walked down the road, already anticipating knocking on number thirty-four.

***

I knocked twice on the door and stepped back, hoping I wouldn't faint or, worse, throw up all over his shoes when he answered the door. That'd be a terrible way to introduce yourself to your brother for the first time.

It wouldn't be the worst first impression I've made on someone, though, but I'll leave that story for another time.

I heard footsteps approach the door and excited voices of young girls. Must be the same ones I saw in the car, the ones I presumed to be my brother's daughters. They would be my nieces. I felt my head spin, and I had to take a couple of deep breaths as a shadow appeared at the door and I heard the latch unlock.

The door opened and he was there, with one of the girls clinging to his leg, little curled blond hair dangling in front of her smiling face. He was smiling too—at least for a moment.

When he saw me, he bent down to the girl and said, "Lisbeth, why don't you go inside and help Mummy with the dinner. Daddy will be back in a minute, there's a good girl."

She giggled and waddle-ran inside.

He stood back and turned to me, closing the door most of the way behind him.

We stared at each other, our eyes locked onto each other. I could definitely see the resemblance, especially in his eyes. His nose was like mine too, just a little broader. I swallowed, trying to clear my dry throat.

"You," he said, his forehead wrinkling with confusion. "From the road. Look, I don't know if this is some silly business…"

I noticed his right eye was bruised and swollen. Had he done that when we both fell?

"I'm sorry," I croaked out, about to turn away. I

was all set to go, my legs already moving, but I forced myself to stay put. I couldn't look at him as I asked, "Are you Michael Fredericks?" It felt odd hearing my own surname.

Over the years, I have gone by a whole host of pseudonyms. Officially, kinda, I was Harley Hill now. Fredericks was the old me, when I was Samantha, when I didn't have a brother. Until now... I reminded myself that throwing up on his shoes was bad and tried to calm my breathing. I was sweating all over and my cheeks were burning.

If I knew I'd be such a wreck, I'd have stayed with Cordi and sung karaoke to 'Burning Ring of Fire'.

"That's me," he said. "What's all this about? Who are you?"

He didn't know. He didn't recognise me. That made it so much worse. I was hoping that when he really looked at me, he would *see*. But then in the photo I had of us, the only photo of us together, I was virtually a newborn.

"I'm..." I couldn't say it. The words died on my tongue.

I heard someone yell inside.

Michael turned to the door. "I won't be a minute, love," he said.

Must be his wife, I thought. The mother of his children, my sister-in-law.

He looked tense now and kept glancing back. "I'm

sorry, but I don't really have the time. If you're selling something, then I'm afraid I'm not interested."

"No," I blurted out, "I'm not selling anything... I'm... oh crap, this is so hard."

"Michael, the dinner's going to burn if you don't hurry up," came an urgent, shrill voice. It startled him, and the muscles in his shoulders tensed. "Whatever it is, I'm not interested in any funny games," he said, turning, opening the door, and heading back inside.

I rushed forward and grabbed his arm.

"I'm your sister!"

He stopped in his tracks, one leg inside the house, the other outside. His body was like stone as if I had just cursed him with some terrible spell.

"I'm your sister Samantha," I said, my voice weak and trembly. I choked down the coming tears and willed myself to be strong.

He turned around to look at me, a whole mess of emotions running through his eyes.

"If I have to tell you again, Michael!" That voice again, with a mean edge to it.

"I'm sorry, I can't do this," he said, shrugging out of my grip. And then he was gone, the door closing behind him with a clunk, and I remained outside, shaking, tears making my vision blurry.

This was far worse than I could have imagined. He *knew* who I was. I saw it in his face. He knew I was telling the truth, yet he left me out here, closed the door on me.

High-pitched shouting came from inside followed by a child crying and then a loud bang. A door slam perhaps. As I turned to leave, I saw movement beyond the curtains of the large bay window. Through a gap I saw Michael and a blond-haired woman arguing in the living room.

She was pointing her finger right in his face, and then she slapped him hard.

I gasped, worried that I was the cause of this argument.

Then she slapped him again, and he cowered away as she continued to hit him.

I couldn't believe what I was seeing. This was more than just an argument between man and wife. But as soon as it started, it was over, the flash of frenzy reducing down to a tense calm. Michael stood up and left the room. His wife, presumably, followed him out, and there was silence again.

I couldn't leave without doing something. I took a business card and pen from my pocket and wrote my cell number on the back with 'Call me, Sam' written on it, hoping that if his wife found it, she might think Sam was a guy. I didn't want to get Michael into more marital problems if I was already the cause of an argument.

With that done, I trudged back to Cordi's car and got in. "Let's get to Oxford Street before the shops close," I said. "We need to get you goth'd up for the club tonight."

"Okay," Cordi said, doing the decent thing and not asking me how it went. I think it was obvious by my body language. I would fill her in on all the details later, but in that moment I turned up the radio as Cordi drove down the road. I looked at the house as we drove by, wondering what was going on in there and what was going on inside Michael's head.

I guessed I just had to wait now.

Just like I had to wait on Cole.

Patience and I weren't exactly tight buddies. It was going to be a long week.

Chapter 15

Despite the issues with my brother and Cole lurking in the back of my mind, I shivered in the queue outside the Black Fang and felt excited. It reminded me of the days when Sapphire and I used to go out clubbing. That was before she got her law degree and became respectable.

"When we approach the doorman, let me do the talking," Jessica said. "I've cleared us, but they'll want to give you newbs a hard time. Just because they can."

"Thanks," I said. "I appreciate you helping us out."

"Don't thank me yet," she said. "You still need to get my grandma's bracelet."

Cordi had barely said a word since we got here. She huddled closed to me, her arm through mine. I found myself sniggering at times, especially on the tube journey as we made our way to Camden, to the club.

We met Jessica on the way. She and I didn't look too dissimilar. The good thing about wearing black jeans and band T-shirts all the time is that they fit right in with a goth club, so I felt quite at home.

Cordi, although having been into The Cure and

similar bands when she was younger, looked entirely uncomfortable in her new outfit and make-up. I gave her the full effect: pale white face, black eyeshadow and heavy mascara, deep red lipstick and neon strips wound through her hair.

She had squeezed herself into skinny black jeans and bought a leather corset top from one of the trendier places in Oxford Street. She looked pretty hot, actually.

We shuffled forward closer to the double black doors that led into the club.

We were basically in a back alley. This place wasn't exactly an elite piece of real estate. But then, by all accounts, Leroy wasn't exactly rolling in the cash these days. The others in the queue were all wearing the same kind of clothes as us.

I was relieved. I had worried that given the cultishness of the club; they'd be wearing something really weird. But then from what Jessica was saying on the train journey, the weirdness didn't start until the early hours.

If things went right, I'd get the bracelet and the information from Leroy we needed before any of that went down. Although I'm open-minded and believe in live and let live, I draw the line at cult events.

"Don't look so worried," I said to Cordi. "Once you get inside and have a drink, you might enjoy yourself. I doubt it's that different to the night we went to the Crobar." That was a little drinking hole in Soho that drew a crowd of metal and rock fans. Cordi and I had a good time there, with her getting more attention than she thought she would.

"I guess," she said. "But everyone here is so young."

"You're not exactly a grannie," I said. "You're only forty."

"Thirty-nine! Going by this lot, I'm old enough to be their mother," she said.

"Okay, we're up," Jessica said, moving forward to talk with the doormen.

They were two great big lumps of muscle dressed in black suits. The one on the left looked like he'd been a sparring partner for Mike Tyson with his broken nose and cauliflower ears. His mate was prettier but no less intimidating with his dark, deep-set eyes beneath an overhanging brow.

They looked at us in the way a pregnant woman looks at a jar of pickles.

I cringed and turned away, not wanting to think about what was going through their heads.

"You two, come through," Broken Nose said, standing aside and opening the door.

The thumping bass of an electronica song blared out. Jessica stepped inside and motioned for us to follow her.

"Here we go," I said. "Keep an eye out for Leroy. If you see him on the dance floor or at the bar, let me know, and I'll sneak up into his office to see if I can find that safe and Jess's bracelet."

"Got it," she said.

We smiled at the doorman as we stepped inside the dark club.

The interior was as unimpressive as the alley we had stood for nearly an hour in.

While Jessica headed to the bar, I took a minute to take my bearings. I always liked to know where the exits and rooms were. One never knew when one might need to make a hasty exit from a sticky situation.

The club had a really simple layout. There was a central dance floor that was already filled with revellers. There must have been about three hundred people in the club already, and there were at least two hundred more outside.

Jessica was right about the ratio. The women outnumbered the men by at least four to one. Lucky boys indeed!

Running along the length of the right wall was the bar.

Three barmaids in skimpy black leather tops were busy running up and down the length of it, serving cocktails and drinks of wild colours. Absinthe and Jägermeister the obvious favourites here, along with vodka and Red Bull by the looks of it.

At the end of the bar there was a black door with a circular window.

I watched as one of the barmaids opened it and went inside.

A few seconds later she was back, carrying a box of drinks. I assumed it was just a storage room. It was unlikely it led anywhere else. That side of the club joined to another building, so there was no exit there.

To the far left of the dance floor, a neon sign indicated the way to the restrooms.

Just before the double doors there was a staircase going up to a second mezzanine floor that overlooked the level below. A wide, expansive glass frontage looked like it held a number of private rooms behind the smoked glass.

Two men wearing black suits came out of a door on the side of those private rooms and descended the staircase. One looked like the doormen while the other one was clearly Dark Horse himself.

It confirmed that he was the man I saw staring into The Page Foundry's window that night. He wore his golden horse pendant around his neck and over a dark mesh shirt. He made his way to the bar, making a beeline for Jessica.

"That's him," I said, but Cordi shook her head, unable to understand what I said.

"It's so loud," Cordi shouted into my ear. "It was never this loud in my day."

"At least you don't need a hearing aid, Grandma Cordelia," I shouted.

She smiled at me and shook her head. "Do you want a drink?"

"No, thanks, I need to keep a clear head. Jessica's with Leroy at the bar already."

"I'll keep an eye on them if you want to do your thing."

"If you can, strike up a conversation with him and see if you can find out anything about this Heruda cult of his. It would be good to know how that fits in with the diary."

"Will do," she said. "Is your cell phone on? If I see Leroy heading your way, I'll call you."

"It's on vibrate," I said. "I doubt I'd hear it with all this bass, but I'll feel it in my pocket."

"Okay, be safe."

"That's a terrible pun," I said.

"Sorry, couldn't help myself."

"Right, enjoy yourself with Leroy and Jess. If I'm not back in a few hours at the most, I'll meet you back at the house. If I get spotted, I'll have to do a runner."

"Let's hope it won't come to that," Cordi said, her voice already hoarse from shouting. I thought about returning a terrible pun with regards to Leroy the Dark Horse, but I was focussing on my task ahead: get into his office and crack his safe.

***

I mingled through the crowd on the dance floor for

a while just so I could watch the comings and goings of the private rooms. It seemed they were currently empty. The big goon who escorted Leroy down had also accompanied a number of women.

I assumed they were up there entertaining Leroy before the start of the night.

After five minutes, no one else had come or gone, so I took that as my opportunity. I casually made my way across to the base of the stairs. I looked over to Cordi.

She caught my gaze and stood in the way between Leroy and me.

His attention was firmly on Jessica, as it had been since she arrived. He was twirling her hair around his finger and whispering something into her ear. She was making vomit faces over his shoulder and urging me to get on with it.

I ducked below the banister as I quickly made my way up the stairs.

The door was locked, but I had brought my lock picks with me, and I was soon inside the dark office. To my relief there was no one waiting for me.

The room was a bachelor's special, with dark furniture, a bed and a sofa, beer fridge and a table that had sprinkles of white powder spotting the surface.

Didn't take a genius to work out what it was.

As I stalked about in the dark, I found the safe easily. It was on the back wall next to the bed. It wasn't even hidden, but given that it was taller and wider than me, I doubted it would be easy to hide. Besides, the dual-locking system on it meant that it wasn't an easy safe to crack.

I knelt down in front of the two dials and called my contact.

'Little Fingers Finnegan' was the best safe cracker in London, if not the country, according to Cole. He'd used him on one of his Robin Hood jobs, relieving a notorious drug dealer from his ill-gotten gains so he could give it to a drugs charity.

It took nearly twenty minutes of going back and forth with Little Fingers to get to the point where I could open the safe. Sweat dripped down my back with anxiety and fear. As each minute passed, I was certain I'd be caught.

I had used a special tool that listened to the mechanism. I fed information back to Little Fingers, and he guided me on what to do. This particular safe didn't require drilling, but the sounds I was listening for were incredibly difficult to make out due to the pounding bass coming up from the floor below.

"Ye should here a wee click when ye turn the dial to zero," Little Fingers said in his thick Irish brogue.

"I hope so," I said. "I'm losing the will to live doing this." My legs were cramped as I kneeled in front of the safe for so long. But when I turned the dial so slowly, I felt the click rather than heard it through the amplifier attached to my other ear.

"Got it," I said.

"Okay, now ye just need to turn both dials to six simultaneously, and that should get ye in."

"Here we go, then."

I did as he instructed, turning the dials slowly and smoothly so that they engaged at the same time. When both dials pointed to six, I heard a deep clunk. I grabbed the horizontal handle and pulled it down. I nearly cheered when it went all the way down, unlocking the safe.

"We're in," I said. "Thanks so much, Finn, I really appreciate it."

"No drama, lass, ye owe me a stout next time ye see me. Now don't get caught now, will ye?"

"I'll try not to. Catch you later."

"Bye, lass."

I put the cell phone back in my jeans' pocket and removed the stethoscope-style amplifier and put that in my jacket pocket. I opened the door and looked inside. I couldn't see much given the darkness of the room. I felt around inside and found a couple of cardboard boxes that were sealed and a bag of powder—must be the cocaine I saw on the table.

But where were Jessica's bracelet and the other trophies?

I leaned further in to get a better look when I heard the door handle to the office rattle. Excited voices, male and female, came from beyond the door. *Crap!*

My phone buzzed in my pocket. It was Leroy!

There was nowhere to hide. The bed was too low to the floor, and the various furniture dotted around the place weren't big enough to hide behind. Even the sofa had a slatted back to it. *Double crap!*

When the door opened, I had but one option.

I ducked down and stepped inside the safe, pulling the door closed. I didn't close it all the way to engage the auto-lock, but just far enough so that it didn't hang open. The shelves were digging into my back, but I managed to squirm far enough back to be a few inches behind the door.

"You're a feisty one, aren't you?" came a voice… Leroy's voice. "Let's see just how feisty, eh?"

A girl giggled and replied, "Take off your clothes. Let me see what the real Dark Horse looks like."

Gag.

Over the thumping bass of the music, I heard Dark Horse and the girl smacking their lips together and panting with frantic passion. Then he howled like a wolf.

I shook my head. What was it with this guy and his fascination with animals? He should have at least whinnied like a horse to stay consistent.

"Take me," the girl said, just before the door to the safe slammed shut.

Oh no… they were actually doing it… against the safe door.

Awkward!

So there I was, hunched into a bizarre shape, hiding inside a large safe, while a howling Horse was 'entertaining' a lady. Well, to be fair, I don't know if she *was* a lady, but let's assume she was out of politeness. Either way, she didn't sound like Jessica.

I stifled a yawn as they kept going on, and on, banging against the safe door.

After a while I got bored and managed to sit down on a shelf and felt something prod me in the buttock. It was a pile of metal items… ooh, trophies! I lit the place with my phone's screen and—Jessica's bracelet!

I pocketed it and continued to wait. Nearly a full thirty minutes later, they had finished. *Finally*!

Although I couldn't be entirely sure if Leroy was still in the room, I was starting to feel claustrophobic and really needed to be out of there. I reached forward and placed the palms of my hands against the door and pushed slowly…

Nothing. No movement at all. I pushed harder, but it wouldn't budge.

The damned door had auto-locked, trapping me inside.

Triple crap!

Chapter 16

Pop quiz. How do you get out of a locked safe from the inside? Answer: you don't.

A hundred ideas came to me, all of them from things I'd seen *MacGyver* do on his show, but seeing as I didn't have a blowtorch, a welder, explosives, or a communications device that could work through five inches of iron, I was all out of ideas.

While those thoughts were going through my head, another terrible realisation hit me: there was limited air inside. My lungs seemed to shrink at that, and I began to sip the air instead of gulping it in with panic.

Easier said than done, of course.

When I started to see coloured stars in my vision, I had to go back to breathing normally. I regretted now not spending more time in the swimming pool developing my breath-holding skills.

When they found my skeleton inside, they would at least recover Jessica's grandma's heirloom. Not much of a comforting thought, however. Not comforting at all.

I was about to panic and start screaming and banging at the door. I figured that I'd find a way of talking myself out of it once someone let me out. But given Leroy's rap sheet, I don't think he was the type to see the funny side of things.

Before the panic completely took over all rational thought, I detected movement outside. I heard the door slam and two male voices talking. And then, making me jump and hold my breath, the dials started turning on the door... the handle moving, the door opening...

It got halfway and stopped.

Dull light from a distant floor lamp flooded inside. I crawled deeper into the shadows like a cockroach as I listened to a tense conversation going on just outside. I saw someone standing just to the right of the safe. Through the gap I could see they were wearing black trousers and shiny shoes with gold buckles on them... must be Leroy.

"I've told you, man, I've got the letter. But it's time to put up or shut up. You have old Simpson's journal or what?"

"Right here. Show me the letter."

I saw Leroy reach into his jacket pocket and reach his arm out.

"You've done well," the other man said. I couldn't see much out of the tiny gap, but the voice was familiar... I'd heard it somewhere recently, but I couldn't quite think of the name.

"As have you," Leroy said, stepping back and facing the door.

I crouched as small as I could into the base of the safe and watched with barely controlled terror as Leroy reached in and dropped a leather-bound book onto one of the shelves.

He turned back to face his co-conspirator. "With that, I doubt it'll be long before I find Dee's Diary," Leroy said. "And then we can all celebrate properly. As long as you have the two million in cash as you've promised."

"Don't worry about the money; it's all in hand. Your job is to find that damned book, and soon. You're not the only one searching for it. Simpson's business partner has hired a pair of busybodies to help locate it."

"You just worry about the cash," Leroy said. "Simpson wasn't far from finding the diary. The location is in that journal of his, in one form or another."

"Don't disappoint me."

"I won't, your Lordship," Leroy replied with sarcasm.

Lordship... of course! *It's Lord Buttsworth.*

I remembered that voice from watching it on the TV the other morning. What on Earth was he doing getting involved with all this? And just like that, it all fell into place: the letter and the journal... both belonged to Simpson.

When Leroy met him on the morning of Simpson's death, he must have given him the letter. Or perhaps Leroy stole it if he was the killer.

As for the journal, that was obvious. Alex had

already confirmed that the chief of police had checked it out of evidence and it had gone missing. Given that Buttsworth was a judge and appeared on TV with the chief, it didn't take Sherlock Holmes to realise that the chief had given him the journal so he could trade for his damning letter and confession of what he did to poor old Skudder.

"A drink?" Leroy said.

"No, I've something I need to attend to. I suggest you remain sober. You've got the diary to find, after all. I don't want you getting sidetracked when we're this close. The secrets inside that damn thing have to be destroyed. It won't just be the House of Lords that will come crashing down—I'll make sure you're implicated too."

"Hey now," Leroy said, "there's no need to get confrontational. Our aims are aligned here. My motivation for the book is as great as yours. You need to trust me."

"I don't trust anyone," Buttsworth said. "I'll call you tomorrow for an update."

"Fine, whatever your Lordship wants. You can see yourself out."

I heard a '*harrumph*' and the door closing with a slam.

Leroy came back to the safe and started to close it. That's when I grabbed the journal and shoulder-charged the door, slamming my entire body against it with as much spring in my coiled, cramped legs as I could manage.

"Ow!" Leroy grunted as the door thudded against his head with a sickening thud.

A second thud followed and I saw his shadow become still. I crept out of the safe and sighed the biggest sigh of relief I've ever had when I saw him sprawled on his back, his hand rubbing his head. His eyes were closed, and I used that opportunity to leap over him and sprint across the room to the door.

Before he could come around, I exited, shut the door behind me, and crab-crawled down the stairs. The music was still blaring, and the security goons were busy attending to the entrance. I sneaked out from the stairs and made my way across the dance floor.

It took a few minutes, but I eventually found Jessica and Cordelia.

They were both dancing by the bar.

Cordi looked like she was really getting into it, grooving to the beat of the electronic music. She had quite a crowd of admiring boys gathered around her. I barged my way through and grabbed her by the arm, shouting into her ear, "I've got the journal and bracelet. We need to go right now."

"I don't need the restroom," she said.

"I mean leave the club. Come on!"

She frowned at me. "I was having a good time."

"If you want to have a good time again, I suggest we

get out of here while we still can." I reached over and pulled on Jessica's arm too in order to get her attention. I nodded my head towards the main doors and mouthed, "I've got your bracelet, and we need to go. Now!"

Her eyes widened as she smiled. She turned away from one guy trying to chat her up and followed Cordi and I as we left the club. Before we exited, I stole a glance behind me and saw Leroy stagger out of his private room, rubbing his head.

"Have a good evening, ladies," Broken Nose said as we hurried down the alley.

When we got out of sight of the club, I handed Jessica her bracelet. She hugged me close to her. "I can't thank you enough, Harley! I thought I'd never see it again. Or I'd have to do something I really couldn't bring myself to in order to get into his good books again."

"I can't breathe," I said.

"Oh, sorry." Jessica let me go, and my poor lungs took in a big gulp of air.

"How did you get it?" Cordi asked. "Was it difficult?"

"It wasn't a stroll in the park, I can tell you that much," I said. "I'll tell you more on the way home. Let's get a cab and get out of here. I don't want to be around to get caught by Leroy."

"What happened?" Cordi asked.

"Long story. Let's just say he's more of a bear with a sore head than a dark horse right now. Come on, I see a cab at the end of the road."

I ran after it, waving my hand. A bald-headed cabbie stuck his head out of the window and gave me the thumbs-up as he waited for us. Cordi could barely walk straight.

"I think those Jägerbombs are getting to me," she said. "I'm getting too old for shots."

"I'll brew us up a nice pot of tea when we get back," I said. I really needed something to help calm my nerves.

We got into the cab and gave him directions. We dropped Jessica off at a tube station and continued on to Cordi's place in Notting Hill. While we drove back, I showed Cordi what else I had found in the safe.

"Is that *the* journal?" she asked, squinting at it with her Jäger-vision.

"Yup, the very same. I remember seeing it in Mr Simpson's clutches when I stumbled across his body."

Oops, I said that a little too loud. The cabbie gave me a quizzical look through his rear-view mirror. I avoided his eye contact and continued to explain to Cordi what I had heard in the safe.

"Buttsworth is everywhere we turn," she whispered. "He's like a bad smell."

"That's one way of putting it," I said. "He definitely warrants a closer look. He's into this up to his ears. The way he was talking, I wouldn't put it past him, especially considering how much he wanted the letter."

"I agree. We'll dig deeper tomorrow. Wait, given that

he did the deal for the letter, it must mean he doesn't know we have a scanned copy of it on Simpson's laptop."

"Handy that," I said. "Gives us leverage. And now we have the journal, we're that bit closer to finding Dee's diary."

"Good work, Harley," Cordi said as she slumped into the seat and started to snore.

We make a good team, I thought. It felt like we finally had our break in the case.

Chapter 17

Day 5

I woke to my alarm on my cell phone just after nine a.m. My back was throbbing. I needed a good long soak in the bath. All that time hiding in the safe had crinkled my back into a pretzel. I groaned like a pensioner and got out of bed.

Despite being quite drunk the night before, Cordi was moving around in the kitchen, and I could smell frying bacon and toast.

My stomach rumbled. I made my way downstairs to the kitchen.

Considering neither of us had hardly stepped into the newly organised office/spare room, I thought it was safe to say that the kitchen was now our *official* headquarters. Which made a lot of sense when you thought about it.

Coffee and cake were the two most important food groups, so it was perfectly logical to have one's place of work where the good stuff was right at hand. And believe me on the coffee and cake theory. It was science!

I read it somewhere on the Internet, so it must be true, right?

"Hey," Cordi said as I shuffled into the bright kitchen. Monty was sitting on the table, his tail doing that twitchy, swishing thing. "How are you feeling? Want a brew?"

"I'd love one, thanks. I'm okay, apart from my back. I might hire a Japanese ninja to chop it into shape later, though. Or perhaps have a herd of elephants stampede over it. I guess I know what it feels like to be a hundred years old."

Cordi laughed as she poured out a mug of coffee. Her hair was looking like something crossed between Albert Einstein and Phil Spector with a hint of eagle-nest chic.

"Hangover?" I asked.

"If you mean do I feel like a resurrected mummy, then yes. But it's nothing bacon and coffee won't fix. Here, get this down you."

Cordi placed a couple of rashers of bacon onto a plate and handed it to me.

Before I could take it, Monty, moving faster than a cat had any right to, launched himself from his squatted position, grabbed a piece of bacon between his teeth, and landed on the floor. He skulked off into the hallway to devour his prize.

I actually preferred to think of it as tithe to keep him happy. I didn't trust that cat and I didn't want to make him unhappy with his puny human servants. His wrath would be terrible and swift.

"Well, there's still one piece left," I said, stabbing it with my fork.

Cordi finished her breakfast and sat at the table. She downed a couple of painkillers with her coffee.

The journal was lying open in front of her. Next to it was a pad of paper and some notes. The sun was streaming through the window over the sink, bathing the kitchen in a golden light. I started to feel a bubble of optimism. It felt like we had made real progress.

"Find anything interesting?" I asked, pointing at the journal and her notebook.

"I can't make head nor tail of it. It's all just gibberish. Some kind of code, I think."

"Given Simpson's interest in the esoteric, I suppose it shouldn't come as a surprise he wanted to secure his findings." I took the journal and flipped through some of the pages.

Cordi was right; it was full of strange symbols and oddly spelled words.

"I know just the man for this," I said, reaching for my cell phone. I calculated the time in Tokyo—they were nine hours ahead of the UK, so it'd be six p.m. over there. *Perfect*. My good buddy, and security-hacker extraordinaire, Henzo would be home from his government job by now. Probably playing one of his online games.

I checked to see if he was on the messenger app we use to stay in touch. His status said he was busy, which meant he was playing games. I sent him a message:

Me: Hey, Henzo, you there? I've got something you'd be interested in.

Two seconds later.

Henzo: Harley! It's early for you. Are you in trouble?

Me: Why do you always assume that?

Henzo: Well, are you?

Me: Kinda, sorta. How'd you fancy getting into a little cryptography?

Henzo: You haven't tried to hack into NASA again, have you? Remember what happened last time? I still owe the ambassador for that one.

Me: Ah, good times, Henzo! But no, it's nothing like that. We're on a case to find a book, and we've found a journal written with some kind of code. If I send you photos of the pages, would you be able to run them through your programs and see if you can decipher it?

Henzo: Sounds fun. I can't start until the morning, though; I'm just about to level up, and my teammates need me to take down this epic boss.

Me: I'm just grateful for whenever, but quicker is better if you can. Things are getting spicy over here. I'll send more details with the photos to fill you in on the case.

Henzo: Cool. Send everything to my secure email account. You still got the password?

Me: Sure, unless you've changed it recently.

Henzo: No, still the old one. No one's managed to hack my new system—yet.

Me: And that's why your government loves you. As do I, you big smelly geek. :)

Henzo: Flattery won't get it done quicker. Now stop slacking and send me those files. I've got a level 70 demon to take down.

Henzo's status reverted to busy.

I took a shot of each page of the journal with my phone, then bundled them into a single file and emailed them across to his secure email account, entering the sixteen-character password he had given to me. When either of us needed to communicate securely, we'd used his proprietary system.

Henzo was as good a hacker and coder as I had ever met. Being the only person to have hacked into the Japanese intelligence services main systems, he was hired immediately.

Along with the photos, I also sent him a copy of the video footage we got from Mr. Cheesebury's alibi. There was just something about it that bugged me, making me think it wasn't legit, but I just couldn't find anything obvious.

If anyone could analyse it and see if there was anything shady going on there, it would be Henzo.

The doorbell rang twice, but before we could get up to answer it, the door opened.

"Good morning. I hope no one is naked. I'm letting myself in, because we don't have time to mess around. Our appointment with the curator at the British Library is in exactly one hour. You know how I feel about time-keeping."

Cordi and I looked at each other and sighed. "Aunt Maggie," we said at the same time.

***

With Maggie's military precision, she had got us out of the house and into her rusting, bright yellow Citroen 2CV in under five minutes, and then we were off, puttering through the busy London roads to the British Library.

The car smelled overwhelmingly of cinnamon. I was sitting in the back, and next to me were six large Tupperware tubs. I lifted the lid on one and saw they were filled with cinnamon rolls covered in icing sugar. I reached for one, unable to resist, and...

Received a whack on my wrist.

"Put that back," Maggie said. "They're for the curator."

"Just one won't hurt," I said. "And I didn't have much of a breakfast—mostly thanks to Monty."

"I don't care," Maggie replied, thankfully turning her attention back to the road. "Besides, a young girl like you ought to take more care of her figure."

"Auntie!" Cordi said with a gasp. "You don't always have to say the things you're thinking. And besides, there's nothing wrong with Harley's figure."

"Of course you would say that, Cordelia. When was the last time you went for a brisk walk or visited a gym? Back in my day, we had to be fit. We had a war on, don't you know?"

Both Cordi and I rolled our eyes. To be fair to Maggie, she had a point. She *had* served in World War II. We didn't really have any standing in that argument—and she knew it. So I reluctantly replaced the lid to the cinnamon rolls and waited for us to arrive at the library.

My hope was the curator would be more generous once he took delivery of his payment. He would have six boxes of them, I'm sure he could spare one measly roll to a starving girl. It'd be the chivalrous thing to do, after all.

***

We waited for Arthur Shackleton, a curator and historian for the British Library, in a dull, stuffy room without windows.

It had the feel of a police interview room with its plastic chairs and cheap wood-effect table. Maggie's cinnamon rolls, in their containers, were stacked on its surface.

Their scent made this whole exercise even more unbearable. My stomach rumbled noisily, but Maggie paid no attention as she clicked and clacked with her knitting needles, making some kind of shapeless garment out of pink and baby blue wool.

I looked at the clock on the wall. Its plain white surface and black hands and numbers reminded me of the clocks in my last school. I remembered most of the time I would have done my work early and just sat, leaning on my desk, waiting for the hands to turn to home time.

I hated waiting. My leg bounced up and down with impatience. Before I had a chance to stand up and go for a walk, the door opened and the smell of dust and Old Spice wafted in.

"I'm sorry for keeping you waiting," the man said, inching his tortoiseshell-rimmed spectacles up onto the bridge of his bloodshot nose.

He blinked his blue-grey eyes rapidly, giving him the aspect of a nervous bird. "Trouble in the archives. One just cannot get the staff these days. Standards have irrecoverably fallen in this day and age, I'm afraid to say."

Cordi and I shared a raised eyebrow. We turned to face Arthur and stood.

We shook hands and introduced ourselves while

Maggie finished her row of knitting. When she was done, she turned her wrinkled, but not unkind, face toward Arthur and smiled wide, genuinely pleased to see him.

I wondered if these two had more going on than just old friends.

"So lovely to see you again, Arthur," Maggie said, kissing his cheek. "I brought you payment in full. I'm sure they'll meet your exacting standards."

Arthur scratched at his goatee beard and lifted the lid off the Tupperware. His face lit up as he breathed the scent in. "Delicious, Margaret. Exceedingly so. A better baker of confections there has never been. I am most honoured."

He replaced the lid and straightened his tweed jacket as though remembering his position. He was a short, squat man, as wide as he was tall, which would be lucky to be over five foot.

Despite his small physical stature, however, he had an aura about him that carried its own gravity. The red silk cravat around his neck hinted at hidden flair within his straight-laced, academic personality.

"I don't want to hold any of you up longer than is necessary, so I suggest we cut straight to the point. Margaret tells me you're looking for the legendary Doomsday Diary. An impressive quest if there has ever been one."

"That's correct," I said, trying my best to be as classy

as he. "Maggie, I mean Margaret, believes you have a pamphlet that might help us in this quest."

"Perhaps," he said. "Please take a seat."

We did as he suggested. We all sat around the table, the cinnamon rolls sadly still encased in their protective shell with not a hint of there being any scoffing of confections any time soon—to my profound disappointment and gastronomical protest.

"Did you find the pamphlet, Arthur?" Maggie asked, setting her knitting aside.

"Indeed I did. It was an easy find. Someone had already checked it from the main archives, and it was in the sorting queue to be returned."

"Do you know by who?" Cordi asked.

"Whom," he said, shaking his head. His curly silver hair dusted the tops of his shoulders. "The reader declined to leave a legible moniker, making the whole situation intolerably obfuscated."

"May we see it?" I asked, eager to get on with things.

"Indeed you may," Arthur said, taking a plastic folder from a file box. He placed it on the table. Within the plastic protective sleeve, a bifold pamphlet of about eight inches long and three wide was wrapped in thin, semi-transparent tissue paper.

Arthur removed a pair of white, cotton gloves from within his tweed jacket's interior pocket and placed them over his small hands. His fingers were like small sausages, but despite that, he handled the pamphlet with surprising care and agility, unfolding the tissue paper as though it were the most fragile thing in the world.

"As far as is concerned, this is the only copy in existence," he said, his voice full of reverie, giving the room a tense, electric atmosphere.

It was as though we were privy to something truly magnificent. An item that connected our contemporary times to a period hundreds of years in the past. I couldn't help but feel the excitement grow within me as he slowly revealed the pamphlet.

We all leaned in, holding our breath so as not to disturb the item, fearful any movement could ruin the fragile paper and turn it all to dust.

"It's surprisingly clear," Cordi said. "I can see every line and curve of Dee's pen."

"Quill," Arthur corrected.

"Arthur, dear, can we look on the inside page?" Maggie asked. "It is there my research suggests there is mention of this Doomsday Diary."

"What the lady wants, the lady gets," Arthur said, carefully opening the document.

Maggie retrieved her magnifying glass from her handbag and leaned in for a closer look. "There," she said, pointing to a line in the middle of a block of handwritten text.

"What does it say?" I asked, unable to decipher the small, intricate lettering.

"Hmm, let me see…" Maggie started as she focused in. "It says… and I'm paraphrasing the old English, 'To a man, the diary is bequeathed. To a man, stout of character, and verve of conviction. For the man will be the bearer, protector, and collective it will remain through the ages, where upon the secrets writ within shall bestow the man great leverage."

I tried to take it all in and parse the meaning, but it didn't seem to help us in discovering the location of the book at all. "Is that it?" I asked, trying not to sound too ungrateful.

Maggie scanned the rest of the document. "That's it," she said. She looked to Arthur. "Does any of that ring any bells for you, Arthur?"

He scratched at his beard for a moment, thinking. "I'm afraid not. If there were perhaps more context, then I could cross-reference with the library's varied databases of records, but the passage is rather vague."

We were all dejected. The early optimism faded away to a sense of disappointment.

While Maggie and Arthur poured over the rest of the wording, I sat back and watched them. They looked so into it, I wondered if I could get away with swiping one of those cinnamon rolls.

But as I began to lean closer to the boxes, I saw something on the plastic protective sleeve that caught my eye: a faded white oval sticker at the top of the sleeve. A crest was printed or perhaps stamped into the oval.

"Can I borrow your magnifying glass for a moment, please, Maggie?" I said.

"What is it, dear?"

"I think I've found something."

Maggie handed me the glass, and I peered through it at the sticker. "That's it," I said. "This is definitely connected to the diary and Simpson."

"How so?" Arthur asked. Cordi and Maggie looked at me expectantly.

"The seal stamped onto this sticker is none other than from the Constable family."

They looked at me with blank expressions.

"Henry Constable the Third was the one who left Simpson the private collection in the first place, remember?" I said, looking at Cordi.

"Yes," she said. "I remember now. Bethany mentioned it."

"That's right," I said. "It means that this was in the same collection. So I'm guessing it was Graham Simpson himself who checked this out initially. Remember Bethany said no one else, other than them and us, knew about the diary? Well, that rules out anyone else other than Simpson from finding it and making the connection."

"I guess you're right," Cordi said, "but it doesn't help us with the diary's location any more than where we already were."

"Perhaps not, but we're on the right track. I think

Simpson might have been closer than Bethany thought. I think we'll find more clues in that journal of his. Arthur, may I take some photos of the pamphlet so we can analyse it more later?"

"As long as you don't use the flash, then please go ahead, my dear."

Like the journal, I snapped multiple pictures of the pamphlet pages on my cell phone so we could dig into it more later. Although there wasn't an obvious clue in the text, there might be some kind of hidden code or message.

Even if there wasn't, it at least pointed us back to Simpson, meaning we were getting closer. Especially as there was no mention of this document in the notes Simpson and Bethany had created on what they had found out already.

I was about to bring up the subject of the cinnamon rolls once I was finished photographing the pages when the door to the small room flew open, and Lord Buttsworth barged in.

Chapter 18

Lord Buttsworth instantly saw the pamphlet and bustled forward, pushing poor old Arthur out of the way as though he was nothing more than a bug on Buttsworth's shoe. "Let me look at that," he barked.

It seemed the lord's bullying antics hadn't stopped at Clifford Skudder.

Maggie looked up at him and frowned. She then hit him on the arm with her handbag, making a loud thudding noise.

"Gerald? Gerald Buttsworth," she said. "How dare you come barging in here like some elephant. Did your dear old mother teach you no manners?"

He whirled round and faced Maggie with a red, angry face.

Cordi and I stood and made to approach him if he tried anything. But we didn't need to. Maggie was made of sterner stuff.

She stood up and faced Lord Buttsworth.

He towered over her. His Dali-esque moustache twitched with anger before his eyes widened and he calmed down. "Oh, Ms. Leroux, I'm sorry, I didn't recognise you," he said, taking a step back, and standing on Arthur's foot.

The historian yelped and staggered away.

"I'm sorry, old chap," Buttsworth said, spinning to face Arthur. "I didn't see you there."

"Quite all right," Arthur said. Which was upper-class British for 'You're a damned oaf and have offended me greatly.' "What do you want? This is a private reading," he said, finding his conviction.

"The same reason as you, I guess," Buttsworth barked again.

"And what might that be?" Maggie said, giving him one of her patented withering stink-eyes.

"I… rem… well, it's confidential of a sorts," he bumbled.

It was a sight to see, watching a billionaire lord be taken down a peg or two by Maggie. I was starting to warm to her, despite her prickly nature. When you wanted to get to the point quickly with no fuss, she was your woman.

"This is about Graham Simpson, isn't it?" Cordi asked.

Buttsworth narrowed his eyes as he turned to face her. "It seems our interests share a mutual outcome," he said, then dropped his eyes to the pamphlet. "Perhaps we can strike a deal, help each other out?"

"You can't buy your way into everything, Gerald," Maggie said. "What would your mother think of you right now? I dare say she'd be spinning in her grave. She brought you up better than this. Just because you have a fancy title now doesn't entitle you to throw your weight around. I knew you when you were still in nappies."

I stifled a laugh as Maggie brought a lord down to the image of a toddler.

"Actually, Gerald, while you're here, perhaps you can answer some of our questions, seeing as you're so eager to help with the Simpson situation."

"Situation?" he asked. "What exactly is this situation you're referring to?"

"I think I shall retire to my break room," Arthur said, wrapping the pamphlet up and replacing it into the storage file. "Let you all have some privacy. Margaret, dear, call me if you need any more of my help. It'll be an honour, as always, and thank you again for the cinnamon rolls; the church fête organisers will be most grateful, I'm sure."

With that, Arthur took the rolls away and left the room.

I felt bereft that I never got a chance to get one. But at least they were going to a good cause. Not that it took away the hunger pangs.

"The situation, Gerald," Maggie began, wagging her finger, "is that you arranged to meet with Graham Simpson the day before he died. In my books, that looks quite suspicious, wouldn't you say? Where were you on that day, Gerald? And don't lie to me; we already know about your confession."

"Confession?" he asked, looking around at us with a terrible effort to look innocent.

"Skudder," I said. "Poor old Skuds."

His face drained of colour and he sat down heavily on Arthur's vacated chair.

"Oh," he said. "You know. I thought I had secured the letter. Did you hear this from that imbecile Leroy?"

"We don't know any Leroy," I said, covering us. I didn't want him to know that we were following up that side of things. We had the advantage in that we had a scan of the letter.

"Well, Gerald? Where were you? Did you kill Graham Simpson to keep your confession quiet?" Maggie asked.

Cordi and I gasped at her courage. Here she was, this little old lady with a white perm and her knitting on the table, straight out asking a billionaire lord if he was a killer. They didn't make people like Maggie anymore.

"I… erm… no, of course not, Ms Leroux, I never met with Simpson."

"That's not what it looks like in your email correspondence with him," Cordi added. "We read the conversation, Lord Buttsworth. You and Graham had agreed to meet the day before his death. Given that it's been ruled as poisoning, that would have given you the opportunity, would it not? The motive is clear, considering the letter only surfaced a week or so ago."

I loved the Cordi-Maggie tag team going on. It was

like bad cop, bad cop.

That didn't make me good cop, though. After knowing Buttsworth was involved with Leroy and this whole Lucarelli business, I found it hard to see him as anything but corrupt and untrustworthy.

"I'm telling you the truth," he said, looking earnest. "Yes, we did arrange to meet. It wasn't just about the letter. I wanted to see him in person, reiterate that I was to blame for poor old Skuds. I wanted him to see that I was genuinely sorry for what happened."

"So why didn't you?" I asked. "If it's true that you didn't meet with him, where were you? Do you have a verifiable alibi?" I was finding the courage from Maggie to ask him the difficult questions. It was quite satisfying seeing a lord squirm under the scrutiny of three women of the general public.

"I was called away on police business," he said. "I've been working with them on a high-profile issue."

"The Lucarelli case?" I asked "I saw it on TV. I know the undercover detective, Cole Lockland. Tell us about it. What's going on there? How does that fit in with Simpson?"

"It doesn't," he said. "It's a separate issue entirely. I was with Lucarelli's family at their private club on the night I was due to meet Graham. And the day of his death, I was with your friend Lockland, dealing with Lucarelli. You saw that for yourself," he said, challenging me to refute his claim.

"Yes," I said, "but can anyone actually vouch for you that you were with them instead of meeting Simpson?"

He stood up and faced me, his great bulk just inches away. Stale cigar smoke tainted his breath. "Why don't you go talk with the Lucarellis and find out for yourself, seeing as you're quite the group of sleuths," he said.

"What can you tell me about Cole and the Sicily issue?"

He just stared at me with burning eyes. "I can tell you nothing. Now stay out of my way, all of you!"

We didn't get a chance to question him further. He left the room in the same blustering manner as he'd entered it.

"Well," Maggie said, "he's far ruder than he was as a child, and that's something."

"How do you know him?" Cordi asked.

"I used to know his mother. We grew up in the same part of East London during the War. His mother and I worked in the same munitions factory. She was my supervisor. Lovely woman. Salt of the earth. Unlike her husband—some member of the gentry. He didn't fight in the War, of course. He worked in the cabinet as a politician with Churchill and his lot. Useless, spineless man."

"Like father, like son," I said.

"Well," Cordi said, "at least we have something to follow up. If Buttsworth's alibi checks out, then we can eliminate him from suspicion. That would only leave

Leroy as our most likely candidate."

I wasn't entirely sure that was true. I was still thinking about Bethany. She had plenty of opportunity to do it, and given that she managed to take control of the business and receive Cheesebury's investment after Simpson's death, she had the motive.

Just because she hired us to find the book and look into his death didn't rule her out completely. I thought it wasn't at all likely, though, but we couldn't be one hundred per cent sure until we had uncovered more evidence.

"There's no way the Lucarellis will talk to us," I said. "They're essentially the Mafia. Given that Lucarelli has been arrested and so publicly, I really doubt they'll just come out and give us information on Buttsworth. They're not going to want to help him out with an alibi considering what he's done to their figurehead."

"You know what we need?" Maggie said. "A nice sit-down and a cup of tea. I can't think straight without a proper brew. Come on, I'll drive us back. We'll come up with a plan later."

Without waiting for us, Maggie grabbed her knitting, opened the door, and left, making us scurry after her.

"Oh, and Harley, dear, I have something for you in the car," Maggie said over her shoulder.

"You do?"

"A box of cinnamon rolls. I made extra because I

know you like my cakes."

"You're my hero," I said.

"That's settled, then," she said. "Back to yours for the evening, Cordelia. I'll stay the night and return home in the morning. But we'll need to stop off at the corner shop on the way, I can't drink that dishwater you call tea. We'll get some proper teabags."

Cordi looked at me with a face of dread.

"Cinnamon rolls!" I whispered. "That gets my vote every time, even if it means spending an evening with Maggie."

"Traitor!"

"Keep up, Cordelia. We don't have all day to dawdle about. The exercise will do you good," Maggie said as she shuffled through the library to the main doors.

Cordi sighed and made a rude face behind her back.

"And stop making faces, Cordelia. It does not suit a woman of your age."

I just giggled and quickened my step to keep up with Maggie's formidable pace.

Chapter 19

Newsflash: I think I'm starting to like Maggie.

To Cordi's horror, it seemed the old girl and I had found a few things in common: baked goods and making Cordi cringe.

There was just something reassuring about her. She was from a bygone era, yet, despite her age, she was still so sharp and skilled. Very little got past her. She had a knack of cutting right to the meat of the potatoes. Behind her dithery, cuddly exterior was a rapier wit and impressive intellect.

The skills she brought to the party were definitely worth having, even if she was often offensive and quick to speak the uncomfortable truth. And those cinnamon rolls were so good, you'd forgive her almost anything to keep them coming.

After an evening of talking about the case and going in circles, I retired early and had a night of fitful sleep. I slept on a futon in the spare room/office so Maggie could have my room.

But that wasn't the source of my bad sleep.

I couldn't stop thinking about Cole.

What Buttsworth had said only increased my anxiety for Cole's safety. I wanted nothing more than to be able to talk to him, find out if he was okay.

Being undercover that deep, infiltrating a Mafia family in Sicily, wasn't exactly a walk in the park. It didn't matter how skilled Cole was; the fact of the matter was that he was swimming with great white sharks.

So many things could go wrong.

A myriad of scenarios came to me during the night, each one worse than the other.

By the time Maggie and Cordi got up, breakfasted, and headed out for the day, I was a tired wreck. I snoozed a bit on the sofa until I found Monty sniffing my ear. I remembered what he did to Lawrence and jerked away.

He'd have to find a snack elsewhere. My ears weren't for chomping.

I yawned and stretched. I paced the room, thinking of what to do.

Henzo was still busy doing his thing with the journal and Cheesebury's alibi video. Cordi and Maggie were doing more research on the Constable family to see if they could find any more connections to the Doomsday Diary.

That left me at a loose end. There were a few options open to me. I could go to the Coffee Tree and try to relax. The only other option, apart from relaxing, which I never found I could do, was to follow up Buttsworth's alibi.

The Lucarellis had a high-end elite club in the West End of London, not that far from Notting Hill.

There was no chance I could get in as a member, and it didn't open until midnight anyway. It was currently eleven a.m. I didn't want to wait that long.

Besides, the Lucarellis weren't the type to just let me question them on their dealings.

I figured I'd go there during the day, and if there was no one there, I'd break in and see if I could find any evidence myself.

If Buttsworth was being honest, then I figured he'd likely be on their security footage for that day. A club like Lucarelli's has cameras everywhere. I had been there once before, with Cole, on slightly shady business—a black market auction.

The location was good for that kind of thing. With all the cameras and the Lucarelli name, no one would dare to try any scams. So breaking and entering wasn't exactly the safest thing to do.

But when I got bored, I lost sight of sensible choices.

I felt frustrated about the case, and if I could find whether Buttsworth's alibi was solid or not, it'd take this case on to another level, at least until I heard back from Henzo.

So that was it. I had decided—today's entertainment was breaking into a notorious criminal family's private club.

To quote Dr. Pepper, 'What's the worst that could happen?'

***

I arrived at Piccadilly Circus station just after noon. I was wearing a peaked cap low over my face, sunglasses and dull grey and black clothes.

I cut an utterly unremarkable vision among the mix of tourists, workers, and people with nothing better to do at midday in the centre of the capital.

Lucarelli's was located down a side street of Regent Street.

At first, I casually walked by, looking into the single dark window, and saw no lights on inside. I tried the door; it was definitely shut. I confirmed by the information outside that it was indeed Members Only and doors opened to members at midnight.

Moving further on, I cut down an alley at the end of the building and found my way to the rear door. I scanned the area; no one else was around. I scouted the place for twenty minutes, making a different route round the front and rear each time at different intervals so nothing looked out of the ordinary.

The place was empty. I was sure of it.

I saw no lights on, heard no voices through the rear door, and no one came or went.

This was it, then. I had to go inside. I'd brought my lock picks with me and started to work on the huge padlock on the rear door. It wasn't the only security they had; there was also a keypad entry system. That didn't faze me, though. Despite what a lot of people thought, they were generally quite routine to bypass.

That was something Cole had taught me in the days when I ran as one of his band of merry men and women. The bypass was achieved with nothing more than a nine-volt battery, some wires, and a little knowledge.

After a few minutes, I managed to pick the padlock and pulled it free. My cell phone, in my back jeans' pocket, buzzed.

Dammit! I was too tense to take a call right now, but if it were Henzo, then it would be worth taking. It might mean I wouldn't have to break in to a Mafia club. That would be a bonus. Making an enemy of brutal criminals wasn't high on my *List Of Things Harley Likes To Do.*

The number was withheld. That meant it could be Henzo. He was too cautious to have his number show up on a call. He routed it through various systems in Russia so he couldn't be traced.

"Henzo?" I asked, accepting the call.

"Um, I think I have the wrong number."

I recognised the voice but couldn't place it. "Who are you looking for?" I asked.

"Sam," he said. "She left me this number, I'm sorry. I must have misdialled."

"No, this is Sam. Is that you, Michael?"

"Yeah, I'm sorry to call out of the blue like this. Is it a bad time to talk?"

"No, it's a great time to talk," I lied, not wanting to put my brother off. Even getting information on Buttsworth paled into insignificance to talking with my brother. I placed the padlock in my pocket and made my way down the alley to stand out in the street so as not to give away my position if anyone happened to come by.

"I'm sorry," he said. "I mean for the way I was at the door. It's just… well, I… oh man, this is so difficult."

"It's okay, I understand. This is super weird for me too. I never believed I'd ever be talking to you, or anyone from my family."

"I know," he said. "It's a difficult situation for everyone, but I wanted to talk to you, explain about last time. I didn't mean to reject you like that. When I first saw you in the road, I knew you weren't just anyone."

"Yeah, that was all quite embarrassing," I said, leaning against a building for support. My legs were shaking. Talking to the first member of my real family was blowing my mind. I wasn't quite thinking straight. I couldn't really think what to say, but he filled in the awkward silence.

"When you came back," he said, "it was a bad time.

I couldn't talk then, my wife and I... well, we're having problems. Big problems, and it was just really bad timing."

I remembered seeing his wife beating on him through the window. I wanted to ask him about that, but I couldn't find the best way to approach it.

"Are you still there, Sam?"

"Yeah, sorry, although call me Harley. I changed my name. I'm Harley Hill now."

"Oh, right, sure, okay, Harley. It's a nice name. It suits you."

"Thanks. So, how have you been?" I asked, not sure what to ask first. I had a million questions rattling around in my head, but now they were out of reach, retreating with a building panic.

"Okay, I guess. I just wanted to say first of all, I never agreed with Mum and Dad's decision to give you away. I fought them all the way over it, but well, then things happened, and it was really the only course of action. I'd like to explain more. Enough time has passed that it's possible now."

"I'd like that," I said, after choking back the tears that were threatening to overwhelm me. "Do you know what happened to our sisters? Are they still around?"

"Not quite... it's really complicated, Sam, sorry, Harley. We ought to meet so I can make more sense. I'm running out of time, I've got to go, she's back."

"Who's back?" I said.

Somewhere in the distance, I heard a door slam and a woman yell out for Michael.

With a panicked voice he said in a hurry, "Crap, I need to go. This'll set her off again... I'll call again soon, when I can."

"Wait," I said. "What's the problem? Why was she hitting you when I visited last time?"

"We're having issues... she's... I'm... she beats me," he said. "I'm sorry, I've got to—"

I heard another door slam, and then the line was cut, leaving me leaning against a building, trying to catch my breath as I pictured what was going on at the other end of the line. He said she beat him... did he mean his wife? Someone else? I considered calling back, but remembered the number was blocked.

For the first time in my life, I felt worried about one of my siblings.

I considered getting on a train to visit him, but what would I say or do? He was still a stranger to me. I didn't know the situation between him and his wife. I couldn't just go stomping in, making things worse.

The frustration built within me. I put the phone back in my pocket and, with renewed purpose, determined I'd get into Lucarelli's and find out whether Buttsworth was a lying sack of crap or not.

As I turned into the alley, I noticed a shadow come from behind me. I felt warm breath on my neck as a pair of hands grabbed me by the shoulders.

Crap!

Chapter 20

They weren't expecting me to react so quickly.

As I spun round, breaking their grip on my shoulders, I was already bringing up my knee into the crotch. I connected perfectly and heard a wheezing 'oomph'.

My assailant collapsed to his knees and clutched his plums while making weird gurgling noises.

"That's what you get when you sneak up on girls, you creep," I said, stepping back, readying to kick him again. I was pretty useful at kung fu, having trained under a top sensei for a few years in my late teens.

Most of that training came back to me in these kinds of situations. My adrenaline was pumping, and just before I had a chance to snap a kick into the scumbag's ribs, he looked up and spoke.

"It's me, Alex. Don't kick me," Alex said, his face red with the pain.

I pulled my kick short, just missing the side of his head.

"What the hell are you doing?" I asked. "You don't just grab someone from behind."

"I won't again, that's for sure."

I helped him to his feet and pulled him further into the alley so no one would see us. He wasn't in uniform, and I wondered if he was working on the Lucarelli case. He was dressed casually in jeans and a leather jacket. He hadn't shaved for a few days and had the beginnings of a beard. It helped accentuate his square jaw, and I had to be honest, it did suit him.

Despite being an intolerable arse, he was indeed very handsome.

Which made kneeing him in the crown jewels both satisfying and disappointing in equal measure.

When he had composed himself, I asked, "What are you doing here, anyway?"

"I could ask you the same question." He pulled the padlock from my hoody top's pocket and glared at me with those blue-grey eyes of his. "You're not picking apples, I know that much. You know this building belongs to the Lucarellis, right?"

"Of course I do. I'm not an idiot—unlike you. I'm breaking in to check on someone's alibi."

"Not the Simpson thing again?"

"Yes, the Simpson thing. It's got a little more interesting of late. I need to know if someone is telling the truth."

"Who is this someone?"

"Does it matter?" I said, getting impatient with Alex and wishing he'd just leave me alone.

"Of course it matters. Do you remember I'm a police detective, right? And you're admitting that your intention is to break and enter private property."

"Are you going to arrest me for assaulting you too?" I cocked an eyebrow and challenged him. I hated it when he pulled this police crap on me. He couldn't just say what he was thinking; he always hid behind this detective persona.

"No, not this time. I think this is a terrible idea. You could really get into some serious crap with this lot."

"What's new?" I asked. "I've faced bigger and badder people than the Lucarellis. I'm breaking in and I'm getting my information. The balls are in your court, as it were, Detective Cobb. Are you arresting me or what?"

He looked around the alley and then back to me.

"How important is this? You know what Cole's doing in Sicily, right?"

"How do you know about that?" I asked.

"Why do you think I got you to the restaurant that night? Cole was undercover but still wanted to talk to you so he could give you that Blackberry. I agreed that I'd get you there so he could run into you."

"You were in on all that? Why didn't you tell me? I thought for all the world that Cole was sleeping with that bimbo."

"We couldn't risk it," he said. "The operation is massive. He'd been working on it for weeks. He wanted to keep you out of it, in case things went bad with

Lucarelli. His family aren't known for playing fair. If they knew you and he were together, you'd be a target and could compromise the operation."

"Oh," I said, feeling stupid for the thoughts I'd had about Cole. "I'm not standing out here any longer talking to you. You're either arresting me or you're not, but I'm going in."

I didn't wait for his answer and returned to the rear of the club. I used a screwdriver to open the casing around the keypad. This exposed the inner workings. With the right application of wires and battery, I got the beep I was looking for and turned the handle.

The door opened.

Alex grabbed my arm.

"Fine," he said. "If you're going in, I'm coming with you. Cole would never forgive me if I just walked away."

"Come on in, then, Mr. Detective Man. You can help me detect whether Buttsworth is full of crap or not."

"Lord Buttsworth? Oh, Harley, you're messing with the wrong people here."

"That means they're the right people to mess with."

I smiled at him, shook his arm loose, and entered the club.

***

I kept my sunglasses on and gave Alex my cap to keep

both of our identities obscured. We crept through the back corridors of the opulent club, looking for an office or somewhere that would have the security camera stuff inside.

The club itself was really high end, featuring expensive flocked wallpaper, lush, crimson carpets (handy to hide bloodstains, I thought grimly), and pictures of various suited men looking all mean and intimidating.

Alex gave me a quick history lesson on the various heads of the Lucarelli family as we continued our search. Throughout, we made sure we kept quiet and moved slowly and deliberately about the place.

We couldn't avoid the cameras, but with our identities obscured, we should be okay. I was searching a stockroom when Alex appeared at the door. "Hey, look sharp, I've found it."

I followed him out and then down yet another corridor. From the outside, you wouldn't have thought the club would have this much space. We hadn't even got to the front of the house yet. Alex disappeared into a room. I entered shortly after.

"Yes, this is it," I said.

A console desk held half a dozen flat-screen monitors in a curving, horizontal direction. A pair of office chairs was set up in front of the desk, presumably where a couple of the Lucarellis' minions would sit and watch proceedings.

"We need to find the tapes for the night before Simpson's death. That's when Buttsworth said he was here, dealing with Lucarelli senior."

"Did he say what time? We can't exactly examine twenty-four hours of footage here."

"He said he was here from eight until midnight."

"Well, at least that gives us a window. Check those filing cabinets, and I'll look over here in the desk drawers."

It took a further ten minutes, but eventually we found a lockbox containing the tapes. I got to show Alex my skills with a pick.

"I don't like the things you know," he said.

"You're a liar. I've seen the way you look at me. Which you can stop doing, by the way. Just because you're helping me doesn't make my opinion of you any better. I'm still one hundred per cent Team Cordi and always will be."

"Do you really want to argue right now or watch that tape?"

"You brought the subject up."

"Be quick. I want to get out of here."

I flicked through the tapes until I found the right date and put it into the tape machine below the monitors. One of them was showing a Windows 8 desktop. Urgh. I hated Windows 8, but needs must. I navigated to the tape drive and started the playback program.

"You keep an eye on those other screens to see if anyone comes," I said. "I'll scan through this and see if

I can find Buttsworth."

Alex sat down in one of the task chairs and spread his legs. I guessed it was so he could ease his bruised apples. Poor baby.

It took a further five minutes of scrolling the tape footage until I found the right time zone. To my annoyance, I did, in fact, see someone appear at the front of the club just after eight p.m. The angle of the camera made it impossible to see their face. They went inside and disappeared off the tape.

Then the angle changed. From this I saw a man in a long coat standing at the bar with his back to the camera. In front of him was one of Lucarelli's enforcers, Little Chilli. Naturally, he wasn't very little. But his hot temper certainly fitted his moniker.

Everyone in the underworld knew of Little Chilli. If you were talking to him, then either you were in serious trouble, or you had dealings with Lucarelli senior.

Chilli was impassively nodding as Long Coat gesticulated. Chilli poured a bottle of whiskey into two tumblers and handed one to his conversation partner. A few seconds later Long Coat handed Chilli a thick envelope.

Chilli opened it and pulled out a thick wedge of cash.

Alex whistled. "That's a serious deal going down," he said.

"Hey, keep an eye on the other monitors. I've got this."

"Okay, okay, is it your guy?"

"I'll know that when he turns around."

I watched for a long five more minutes, all the while willing Long Coat to turn around so I could see his face. As each second ticked by, I got more and more nervous as doubts set in. Perhaps I wouldn't get the answers I was seeking, and then we'd be back at square one again.

I scrolled the video forward and saw Long Coat start to move, so I stopped the tape and let it play at normal speed. "Here it comes," I said. "He's turning around... any second..."

From behind me I heard the sound of a gun hammer being cocked, and then everything went dark as something was thrown over my head. My hands were dragged behind my back.

I heard Alex call out and struggle before a loud thud silenced him. I tried to kick out, but whoever had hold of me was too strong. Something hard struck the back of my head, sending a bolt of pain through my skull and rattling my teeth. I felt light-headed and collapsed to the floor, unable to breathe through the pain.

"Take them into the stockroom," an Italian-accented voice said. "I'll call Buttsworth; he'll want to deal with this personally." They were the last words I heard. I vaguely remembered being dragged out; by then, everything was black and muffled.

Chapter 21

I didn't know how long I had been out, but my head was killing me.

My neck was stiff and I felt pain all over. My arms were cuffed behind my back, and a sack of some kind was tied over my head. I could still breathe through the fabric, but I couldn't see anything.

"Alex, are you there?" I said with a strained whisper. No answer.

I reminded myself not to panic. I had to stay calm and think my way out of this. I had been in worse situations and got out of them. *Like the safe.*

Only this time, I didn't want to wait for someone else. If they came, I knew I'd likely be finished. I didn't trust Buttsworth as far as I could throw him. He'd have me killed. I had no doubt about that.

First things first—get my bearings, I thought. I righted myself and sat up. I rocked forward onto my knees and shuffled about. I bumped into various shelving units and tables. I remembered they mentioned a stockroom.

In my exploration I came across another lump on the floor. Alex! I nudged him with my knee. "Alex, wake up. It's me, Harley. Are you okay?"

I hoped they hadn't killed him. A blow to the head could have easily...

"Harley? What's going on?" Alex finally said, breaking the tense silence. He sounded drunk or sleepy.

"We're in the stockroom," I said. "You've been cuffed and bagged. I think it was Little Chilli and his goons. They're calling Buttsworth. He's definitely involved with them beyond the Lucarelli case. We've got to get out of here."

"My gun..." he said. "Crap, it was on the desk. Are you okay?"

"I've been better," I said. "But I can move if I ignore the pain. Listen, my hands are cuffed. I can get out of them if I can find something to fit into the lock."

"A pen?" he asked.

"That might do it."

"In my jacket pocket."

"Okay, stay there. I'm going to turn around and try to find it. I can only move my hands a few inches, so you'll have to move into position."

It was a difficult manoeuvre, but after a fashion I managed to get the tips of my fingers into the pocket and pull out the pen. I removed the nib and ink barrel and used that to try to pick the lock.

I had very little mobility and room, and I kept dropping the pen.

"Alex, turn around and hold the cuffs for me while I

try to pick it."

That was much better. With our backs to each other, he held my cuffs steady and I got to work. It was harder using the pen as it was made of plastic and didn't translate the feel of the lock mechanism as well as a proper pick.

"How are you doing?" Alex asked. "I'm cramping up."

"One more moment… I just need to twist it and…" I heard the click, and the cuffs came loose. "There."

It felt so good to be free of the cuffs. I rubbed my wrist and rolled my shoulders to rid myself of the aches and cramps. I hurt all over, but the adrenaline rush and the fear kept me moving on. I removed the sack from my head and quickly got to work releasing Alex from his cuffs.

Our legs were bound by rope so that was easy to deal with.

"Let's get out of here," I said. "Before they come back."

"Can you remember the way?" he asked.

"Right out of here," I said.

"That's to the camera room; we need to go left."

"I'm not leaving without proof." I opened the door an inch and listened. I could hear voices coming from further down the corridor beyond the camera room. Without waiting for Alex, knowing he would object, I slipped out and tiptoed to the camera room.

Poking my head round, I made sure it was empty before entering.

My cell phone was on the floor. I picked it up and placed it back in my pocket. I had a look for Alex's gun, but it had been taken. The tape was gone too. *Crappity crap!* When would I catch a break?

I was about to return to Alex when I heard one of the goons say from the end of the corridor, "Buttsworth's here. Get Chilli."

"You get him."

"Fine, you lazy bum."

A minute later I heard Buttsworth's unmistakable voice.

"Chilli, I got here as soon as I could. A girl, you say?"

"Yeah. They're out back."

I moved back away from the door and looked on the monitors. I saw Buttsworth standing there with Chilli. I got the lay of the room they were standing in and committed it to memory. It looked like a regular office with a large wooden desk and standing filing cabinets. Chilli was sitting behind the desk, his feet on the desktop. Buttsworth paced opposite.

A third man was standing in the corner, his hands in his pockets, all casual and looking almost uninterested in the whole thing. That told me all I needed to know about how these guys felt about dealing with people. This was routine for them.

I moved back to the door and crept out into the

hallway. Alex poked his head out of the stockroom. I quickly moved across. "Buttsworth's here. I found my phone."

"So? Let's get out of here while we still can."

"Not a chance," I whispered back. "I can record them… for evidence. How'd you like to be the one to bust Buttsworth for corruption, fraud, and who knows what else?"

He thought about it for a moment. "Let me find a weapon."

He went back into the stockroom and I followed, not wanting to be too exposed by standing outside in the hallway.

"This will do," Alex said, lifting an empty vodka bottle.

"Follow me," I said.

I led Alex out and down the hallway until we came to the office. We could hear the voices loud and clear. The door was closed about three-quarters. I could only see the shadows of the men inside on the floor.

"Someone's up ahead," Alex whispered in my ear, pointing to the end of the corridor where it came to the bar area. He was right. Someone was standing there, looking out into the club, one hand in his pocket, the other holding a cigarette. "Wait here," Alex said, slowly stepping past the office.

He approached the goon with the stealth of a panther and struck him hard on the back of the head. There was only a slight 'thud' noise. The bottle didn't smash like it does in the movies. The goon slumped to the ground, and Alex caught him with his free hand to make his fall as quiet as possible. He took a gun from beneath his suit jacket and returned to me, leaving the bottle behind.

"Phone," he mouthed, gesturing me to give mine to him.

I handed it over, and he sent a text. "Cavalry," he mouthed.

He handed it back to me, and I made sure it was still on silent as I swiped the touchscreen until I found the voice-recording app. I activated it and held it toward the door.

"What are you going to do with the bodies?" Buttsworth asked.

"Don't worry about it; we have disposal strategies for such events."

"How much will it cost me?" he asked.

"The standard rate."

"Cash again like last time," Buttsworth said. And I nearly fist-pumped that I got that recorded.

"That'll be fine," Chilli said. "But before we get to that, there's the Sicily issue to discuss."

"I thought we had already agreed on a deal with that?" Buttsworth said. "I'd expose Lockland and forward the details to your guys over there to deal with him and Gianni. Have I not arranged that as I said I would?"

"Oh, you did, yeah, that's all going down tonight. It's going to be a tragedy, but hey, whatya gonna do, eh? Luckily, Gianni has me to take over the family. Ain't that right, Mario?"

"Yes, boss," the other goon said.

My hand was shaking. Not through the effort of holding up the phone, but the realisation that Cole and Gianni were being set up.

They weren't over there to infiltrate the Mafia for Buttsworth's case; they were being sent there to be slaughtered so Chilli could become the new boss.

I was sick to my stomach, and before I knew what I was doing, I put the phone in my pocket and rushed into the office, my hands balled into tight fists.

***

They didn't see me coming. I covered the distance in just three steps and threw all my force and weight into the back of Buttsworth.

The impact pushed him and the desk into Chilli. He yelled out as the desk struck him in the chest, pinning him to the wall behind him. The goon to his right went wide-eyed as he tried to figure out what was happening.

I was already moving back, readying to launch myself at Chilli, when Alex pulled me back and stepped forward, pointing the gun at the goon.

"Drop your gun, scumbag," Alex growled as he cocked the hammer.

"Don't you dare move," I said to Buttsworth. He was still lying face down on the desk. I grabbed a paper-weight and brought it high. He saw what I was going to do and remained still even as his face distorted with anger.

Chilli's face was puffing with fury as he was still stuck. I leaned against the desk so he couldn't move. The goon did as Alex said and dropped his gun.

"What ya doing?" Chilli bellowed. "Get him!"

"Sorry, boss," the goon said, shrugging his shoulders and pointing to Alex's gun.

"You, turn around and put your hands on your head," Alex said to the goon, who did as he was instructed. Alex brought the butt of the gun down hard on the back of his head, knocking him to the ground.

I rushed round and picked up the other gun just as Alex's bottle-victim staggered into the room with a confused expression on his face. I aimed the gun at him and yelled at him to stop and get to his knees.

Alex pulled the cuffs we had removed earlier from his jeans pocket and cuffed the two goons. We then turned our attention to Buttsworth and Chilli.

"You'll both pay for this," Buttsworth said, turning to face us. "You'll regret this, I swear it. I'll bury both of you. You don't know who you're dealing with."

"He's right," Chilli said, having given up trying to excavate his large frame from the desk. "You won't get away with this. It's just a matter of time."

"Is that so?" Alex said. "Lord Buttsworth, I'm arresting you on suspicion of corruption, perverting the course of justice, conspiracy to murder—"

"You fool," Buttsworth said. "I didn't kill Simpson. Check the tape yourself. You'll see me and Chilli talking on the night I said I was."

While Alex held the two at gunpoint, I took the tape from Buttsworth and returned to the camera room. And he was right. I watched further beyond the moment we were discovered, and I saw him turn to face the camera—it was him all right. There was no mistaking it.

I went back to the office. "He's right; his alibi checks out."

"I wasn't just talking about Simpson," Alex said, still pointing the gun. "I was talking about Lockland and Lucarelli. We heard everything, Buttsworth."

I removed my cell phone and played back the recording of him confessing.

He remained still as though he had turned to stone. The colour drained from his face and he slumped to the desk, a broken man. He dropped his head into his hands. "You've got me," he said, with a shrug. "There's no denying it."

"Then help me help you," Alex said.

I didn't know what he meant, but he continued. "I'll promise you a deal right now. You help us get Cole out alive and we'll drop the charge of conspiracy to murder—as long as you give evidence against Chilli and the Lucarelli family."

Buttsworth stood up and turned to face Chilli, who couldn't speak he was so angry. His face was bright red, and I knew he'd kill Buttsworth if he had a chance.

"It's a deal, Detective Cobb," Buttsworth said. "I'll give you everything I know about Lockland. If you call Interpol right away, there might still be time to get him and Gianni out of there. The hit was due to go down later today—on Chilli's orders."

By the time Alex got off my phone with Interpol, we heard shouts and banging coming from the front and the rear of the club. A group of fifteen armed police came crashing in.

Alex spoke with the officer in charge and told him everything. The armed police escorted out the goons, Chilli, and Buttsworth.

As he passed me, Buttsworth said, "I was heartbroken about Simpo. I truly was. I sincerely hope you find the killer."

"So you admit it wasn't suicide," I said.

"Indeed. I only covered that up to stop the truth about what I did coming out. I couldn't afford for the police to start poking around into Simpo's life. But I guess I didn't anticipate someone like you coming along and messing with my plans."

"Consider it a public duty," I said.

"It's never too late to make a deal," he said, his face hopeful.

"I would never touch your filthy money." And to the officer holding him, I said, "You can take him away now. For good."

***

After Alex and I had given our statements to the officer in charge, they dropped us off back at Cordi's place. I called her to let her know what had happened. When we arrived, Maggie was there too.

I explained everything about Buttsworth and how his alibi worked out. I didn't tell them everything about Cole, because I was still nervously waiting for an update from Interpol. Alex had recovered his phone from the club and made further inquiries, but there was no update yet.

As I sat there at the kitchen table, drinking coffee, my phone alerted me to an incoming email. I checked it and saw that it was from Henzo. It read:

Harley,

Hey, girl, nice puzzle that journal. Had me taxed for

a good few hours. The cryptologist was very clever, but not quite clever enough. I've included a fully decoded transcript of the journal for you in an attachment to this email. I don't really understand what it all means, but you'll have to tell me the story surrounding this, as it's very intriguing.

Oh, and the video of Mr. Cheesebury—seems legit to me. At least file-wise. I can't find any trace of there being any editing or altering of it. What you see on the footage is what happened.

Hope that helps. Looking forward to hearing all about this one when you sovle it.

Your stupid geek friend,

Henzo.

I came out of the email message and was about to load up the transcript when Monty pounced from nowhere and landed on the kitchen table with a thud.

He *merped* loudly in my face and pawed the screen on my phone.

"Hey, watch it, fur ball," I said.

He meowed for the second time and pawed the phone's screen, bringing up Henzo's email again. That's when I noticed it. Once I moved Monty's large furry butt out of my face, I saw the spelling mistake in his email.

I reread the second from last line. He had misspelled 'solve'. He had 'l' and the 'v' round the wrong way...

sovle, instead of *solve*. The 'l' was on the wrong side.

Wrong side! Of course! How did I not see it before?

"Monty, you're a bona fide genius!"

He just grumbled and flopped off the table; then he proceeded to preen himself.

Even before I checked out the decoded journal, I reached over the table for the laptop and opened the lid. I navigated to the folder holding all our research for the case and watched the security camera footage of Mr. Cheesebury again.

It all started to make sense.

I read the transcript of the decoded journal, absorbing the words faster and faster as a new theory blossomed into fruition. When I finished the transcript, I stood up so suddenly, the chair fell back and clattered against the kitchen floor.

Monty meowed and darted into the hallway.

"Yes!" I shouted. "I've figured it out!"

Cordi and Maggie poked their heads through the door.

"What is it?" they said.

"I've solved it… it all makes sense now. Come on, we've got to get to The Page Foundry right away."

***

Alex, Cordi, Maggie, and I raced over to The Page Foundry in Alex's car. It only took a few minutes. I burst through the door to find Bethany, Mr. Cheesebury, and Leroy, aka Dark Horse, all standing in the middle of the shop, arguing. Alex, Cordi and Maggie soon followed me.

Everyone, on both sides, was staring at me.

"They are the killer," I said, pointing to the perpetrator.

Chapter 22

I moved forward, cell phone in hand, and pointed again to the killer.

"You thought you could get away with it, and you nearly almost did," I said. "But I figured it out. You, Mr. Cheesebury, are Mr. Simpson's killer!"

There was an audible gasp from everyone else in the shop, not least Bethany, who recoiled from Cheesebury as though he had the plague. She reached for a handkerchief in the breast pocket of her lime green suit jacket.

Leroy shook his head in disbelief and backed away from Cheesebury. "You! You slimy… two-bit…"

"This is preposterous!" Mr. Cheesebury said, straightening his tweed tie. "How dare you come in here like this and accuse me of such a thing. Do you have any evidence for this wild, unsubstantiated claim?"

I backed away from him and joined Alex, Cordi and Maggie.

"Do you?" Maggie asked.

"Harley, tell us, what's going on?" Cordi asked.

"Mr. Cheesebury," I said. "Can you come here, please? I'd like to show you something."

He looked at me quizzically. "What ever for."

"Do you want me to show you why I think you're a killer? As well as a liar and a thief?"

"I'll have none of this!" he said, exploding with frustration. He stalked toward me, limping as he came closer. Alex stepped forward and stopped him in his tracks.

"Let's all just calm down," Alex said, glaring up at Mr. Cheesebury's long face. Alex was not exactly a short man, but the older man was at least half a foot taller with his long, thin frame.

"Did you notice that?" I said to everyone, pointing to his right leg. "The way he limped?"

Bethany, seemingly having composed herself, looked confused. "Of course, he has a prosthetic."

"A fox-hunting accident when I was a teenager," he said. "I don't see what that's got to do with any of this."

"It has everything to do with everything," I replied. I looked over to Leroy, who was fidgeting nervously by a stack of books. "Leroy, you can go, if you want. I know it's not you."

"I want to watch the show," he said. "As unlikely as it sounds, given my record, Graham Simpson and I were friends. We helped each other on research projects."

"Oh?" Cordi said. "How so?"

"When I was in prison, Graham visited me. Well, not me specifically to begin with. He was the head of a book program within the prison. He managed a small library and would help us talk about and critique books. All part of the rehabilitation process. Giving us reading and critical skills. It was then that we learned we had a common interest: the occult and the works and theories of John Dee."

"Huh," I said. "That's all rather unexpected."

"So you see," Mr. Cheesebury said, "this man clearly has more of an interest in Simpson and that damned diary than I do. If anyone killed Simpson, it's him. He's a violent criminal, after all!"

"Was," Leroy corrected. "Like Graham, I too wanted to find the book, and when I heard his death was ruled as suicide, I knew it was rubbish, so I started digging into things myself. Turns out, a lord is involved."

It was my turn to say, "Was." I explained what happened with him.

"So with all that said," Maggie exclaimed, "how does this fool of a man's limp have anything to do with Simpson's death?"

"Alex, would you mind doing the honours? I don't want him going anywhere when I show this."

Alex nodded and grabbed Mr. Cheesebury by the arm.

Everyone surrounded me in a half circle. I pulled out my phone and loaded Mr. Cheesebury's alibi video onto the screen and pressed play. "Watch the video," I said. "It's all right there."

Cheesebury had a smug look on his face as the video

played.

It showed him arriving at a large house in his black Jaguar, getting out and going inside for about ten minutes. He then came out, carrying a box of books, which he placed into the back of his car before driving off.

"See," Mr. Cheesebury said, pointing at the video. "How could I be there, a hundred miles outside of London, and be here at the same time to kill poor Mr. Simpson?"

"Yes," Bethany said. "How?"

Everyone else was looking at me with confusion, apart from Maggie. She tapped me on the shoulder and smiled at me. "This one's a real smart cookie, Cordelia. You'd do well to give her a pay rise. You don't want to lose her."

Cordi, Leroy and Alex looked at me with expressions of confusion. "I don't get it," Cordi said. "What does this prove?"

"The limp, woman, look at the limp," Maggie said, rolling her eyes.

I replayed it.

"It's the wrong side!" Cordi finally said. "He's limping on the left leg, not the right."

"What do you make of that, Mr. Cheesebury?" I said.

"I… I… well… um…" he blustered, unable to find his words.

I continued. "You had someone drive your car to

the house. You had them dress as you, but whoever it was had forgotten to make sure his limp was correct. With an imposter creating this so-called alibi of yours, it freed you up to visit Mr. Simpson, whereupon you poisoned his drink." I turned to Alex. "Now that Buttsworth isn't obscuring the case, I'd suggest going through the crime scene again. I'm sure you'll find the source of the poison."

I walked over to the basement door.

"This is crazy," Mr. Cheesebury said. "I demand a lawyer!"

"I haven't arrested you yet," Alex said.

"And I'm not finished with you either," I added. "You see, this basement door was locked with a police-issue padlock. I saw it when I came back last time. But as you can see, there is no such lock anymore, and the basement door can freely"—I pulled the handle—"open. Now, this is where it really gets interesting." I returned to the others.

I had their full attention as I showed them the transcript of the journal.

"The journal that we all believed belonged to Mr. Simpson actually belonged to the previous owner of the collection, Mr. Simpson's benefactor."

"Mr. Constable?" Bethany asked.

"That's the one," I said, pointing to a scanned image of a family seal stamped onto the front page of the journal. "I saw this same seal on a pamphlet from the British Library. It was then that I started to wonder about the journal. Once my friend decrypted the code, it all fell into place."

For dramatic effect, I walked slowly around the room, milking it for as much as I could. I didn't get a lot of moments like this, so I made sure to enjoy it.

"The journal was a filing system," I said. "When I first found Mr. Simpson's body in the vault, I had seen a number of very old boxes with numbers and letters stamped on the front. These boxes held the thousands of items that Mr. Simpson was so slowly and meticulously recording and researching."

"How does that fit in with all of this?" Leroy asked.

"The Doomsday Diary," I said. "Was here all the time, among Constable's vast collection. Wasn't it, Mr. Cheesebury?"

"Preposterous!" he said again, but I could see it in his eyes: he knew that I knew.

"The boxes correspond to the journal's decrypted filing system. The Doomsday Diary, according to this"—I held up the transcript on my phone—"should be in box XB19. Let's take a look, shall we? Mr. Cheesebury, if you would be so kind as to go first."

Bethany brought a number of flashlights for us, and we all filed into the vault, Alex never letting go of Cheesebury. The boxes were piled high and arranged in order as I remembered. They created a kind of maze with narrow passages.

Eventually we came to box XB19.

I shined my flashlight onto the ground just in front of the pile of boxes. "It looks pretty clear of dust here," I said. "But not as you go further. It seems to me that someone has been here quite recently."

Cheesebury grumbled under his breath.

Leroy helped me remove the boxes that sat atop XB19.

Everyone peered inside the now accessible box.

"It's empty," Bethany said. "The diary isn't there."

"Exactly," I said. "Someone… or more accurately, Mr. Cheesebury figured it out and took the book. Now, how could someone work it out with the decoded journal? Easy, Mr. Simpson had made a copy and the killer had stolen the copy."

"How do you know?" Bethany said.

"Because he scanned the copies onto his laptop. One thing Mr. Simpson liked, I have come to realise, is backups."

"If I stole the book as you claim," Cheesebury said, "then where is it? You can't convict me of theft of an item that doesn't exist."

"It does exist," I said, "and I know exactly where it is." I turned to Alex and the others. "Anyone fancy a road trip to The Book Vault?"

Chapter 23

An hour and a half later, we arrived at Mr. Cheesebury's store.

He protested the entire way, but even then, he still thought he had one over me, so sure of himself that he was too clever.

We had dropped Leroy off at the train station, as he had important club business to attend to. I promised Alex that he wasn't the thief or murderer, and that he was free to go. I also wanted him to wait until now before he officially called in the arrest.

We gathered in Mr. Cheesebury's private office.

"Nice room," Alex said.

I could still smell the spilled brandy, and really, that was where it all had started. If it wasn't for that accident, then I'm not sure I would have had the right thoughts in mind to have seen all the clues clearly enough.

"Get on with it, then," Cheesebury said.

Without wasting anymore time, I strode across to the drink's globe and lifted its lid. I put my hand down the back and... there it was! I lifted it out and showed it to everyone.

"I present John Dee's Doomsday Diary."

Bethany and Cordi gasped with surprise.

Cheesebury groaned and hung his head.

"How did you know?" Maggie asked.

"It was a complete accident, wasn't it, Mr. Cheesebury? You remember, I'm sure, I broke your executive toy and I slipped on a steel ball, knocking your drinks globe over."

"Quite," he said, dejected.

"I didn't think much of it at the time," I added. "But I noticed there was quiet a large gap behind the whisky bottles. It looked odd, but nothing to really cause any real suspicion. Of course, once I saw the video and realised it was fake, my brain seemed to remember all these little details. Like this one, for instance." I picked up the Sudoku book I had noticed on the desk before.

"This is what made me realise someone else, other than my friend, had decoded the journal—or more accurately, Mr. Simpson's copy." I flicked to the back of the book where the seemingly impossible Sudoku puzzles were. "See," I said, showing everyone. "He's completed every single one—without a mistake. Mr. Cheesebury is adept at puzzle solving. Which made him the perfect candidate to solve Constable's encrypted filing system."

He sighed and let his chest fall with resignation. "You're right, about everything. I can't deny it."

Bethany stepped away as the reality finally dawned on her that her old friend was a killer and a thief.

"Why?" she asked, with a keening voice. "Why all of this?"

"The diary," he said, shaking his fist. "It was all for the diary! I had to have it. I had learned of it when I was just a boy. It was the entire reason why I got into literature and book dealing. My entire adult life I've searched for that book.

"For years, I had worked alongside Graham on Constable's library, knowing it was there, somewhere, but back then we didn't even really know what we were looking for. As the years went by, I resented Graham. Why did he get the collection and not me? I was closer to old Constable. I had put in far more hours on his academic projects than him. That collection and the Doomsday Diary should rightly be mine!"

"So you killed him," Bethany said. "You killed that poor, sweet man for your own greed. You could have shared the discovery! You could have worked on it together." She broke down and buried her face into a handkerchief.

Cordi and Maggie consoled her.

"I tried," Cheesebury said. "But he wouldn't listen. He was stubborn! You know that. It's why he wouldn't accept my investment when you were so close to going bankrupt. The old fool was too short-sighted."

"I hope you burn in hell," Bethany said. "Please, someone, just take him away."

Alex dragged him out of the office and called in the

arrest.

While we waited for the police to arrive, we opened the Doomsday Diary and discovered why it was so dangerous if it ever got out into the public.

Chapter 24

Day 7

Cordi and I were sat in the living room, quietly drinking tea, taking in the warmth of the fireplace. Monty was curled up in front of it, warming his fur. He purred contentedly, no doubt thinking the success of the case was all down to him and his perfectly timed paw swipe.

I was starting to change my opinion on him. Perhaps he wasn't so bad after all. Sure, he often stole my breakfast, but if he was going to help solve cases, I was happy to share my food with him.

As for Cordi and I, neither of us slept at all well after the previous day's exploits. I had been up all night waiting on news about Cole.

I didn't understand why Interpol were being so quiet about it. Alex called them a dozen times to get some information on what was happening. They kept saying they were working on it and couldn't tell us anything at this time.

On top of that, I was worried for my brother. The

phone call had come back to me after all the excitement at Lucarelli's.

He sounded genuinely concerned, and perhaps scared?

I know domestic abuse isn't solely limited to men on women, but it's so rare to hear it the other way around. It's hard to know exactly how to react or what to say. I couldn't call him, and I didn't want to make matters worse by visiting him.

Like Cole's situation, I had to wait.

The anxiety burrowed into my mind and made my sleep fractured. I felt exhausted and could do nothing but sit there on the sofa, sipping tea, and staring at the cause of Mr. Simpson's death: the Doomsday Diary.

To look at it, you wouldn't think such a thing could be damaging. Sure, it looked old with its cracked brown leather binding and yellowing paper, but it was the words inside that were the real cause of the trouble.

John Dee was indeed a very clever man with lots of potentially explosive secrets on some of the world's most powerful monarchies and families—many of whom were now some of the world's biggest and most influential bankers and industrialists.

"It might not have brought down society as we know it yet," I said, "but it's ruined enough lives already."

"I agree," Cordi said. "So what do you want to do with it?"

There were a few options: release it to the public

and let the revelations do what they will; give it to the police—Alex had given it to us to make that decision; sell it to a library or museum, or...

"I think we have to destroy it," I said. "We can have Alex release a statement saying that it got damaged in an accident or something. The important thing is no one else seeks it out. We can't allow the secrets to get out. We've already had enough bloodshed over it."

Cordi ran a hand through her long brown hair and exhaled. "It doesn't feel right to destroy something so old and penned by someone so famous. But... I think you're right. I was up all night last night running the ramifications through my mind. It would cause so much trouble for so many people, and given how long ago this was written, I don't think it's fair for people of today to pay for the sins of their ancestors."

I looked at Cordi. "Are you sure about this, then? We're going to destroy it."

"Yes. I can't see any other option."

"Okay."

Without wasting any more time thinking about it, I placed my teacup on the coffee table and stood up from the sofa. I grabbed the weighty tome and strode across the living room to the fireplace. The flames were already burning hot, the logs turning black, popping and crackling within the fire.

I bent down and scratched Monty behind his little, furry ears. His purr grew louder as he looked up at me with his soulful yellow eyes. "Should I burn it, Monty?" I asked.

Mreow.

"I'll take that as a yes, then."

Monty watched me place the book into the fire. I pushed it further in with a poker and watched as the flames flickered and grew brighter as the old, dry paper ignited immediately.

Within seconds, the pages and the binding were turning black and curling with the flames' touch.

The tension in my guts eased. I knew I had done the right thing. It was a relic, a time bomb of which no good could come. "That's that, then," I said, settling back down on the sofa as Cordi and I both sat in silence and watched a centuries-old book burn to ashes.

"We can't tell anyone about what we read," I said.

"Pinkie swear," Cordi said, holding out her pinkie finger. I hooked mine around hers, and we made the oath.

"I'm so tired," I said. "I could sleep for a week."

"I know how you feel. But don't fall asleep yet; we've still got some of Maggie's cinnamon rolls left. You want to help me finish them?"

"Do bears poop in the woods?" I said, smiling.

"I'll go and get them. You rest up."

"Thanks, Cordi."

I watched her leave the room and head for the kitchen. I closed my eyes for a moment and was about to drift off when I heard an urgent knock on the door. Groaning, I got up and went to see who it was.

Being so tired, I didn't even bother with the spyhole; I just opened the door and squinted out into a bright autumnal day. I blinked away the sleep in my eyes and stifled a yawn. That's when I saw who it was. My body and mind woke instantly.

"Cole!" I screamed, wrapping my arms around his neck. My momentum nearly sent him crashing down the steps.

"Whoa, easy," he said, leaning forward and wrapping his arms around me.

"I was so worried," I said, my face still pressed against his neck. "I thought you were… thought they…"

"It takes more than a Mafia family to get the better of me. I'm sorry for not calling sooner. I couldn't trust the phone line. Interpol got Gianni and me out of there, but there's a huge fallout still going on. I had to remain quiet. The Mafia have ears everywhere."

"I'm just so glad you're back and safe," I said, finally letting go and standing back so I could get a good look at him. He had an ugly, purple bruise above his right eye. I touched it gently with my fingertips. "What did they do to you?"

"I'll tell you over a cup of tea. One thing about the Italians is they're obsessed with coffee. I haven't had a decent cup of tea in ages."

I kissed him, unable to resist after not seeing him

for all this time. He responded, pulling me in tight and returning my affections. When we broke away, we were both breathless.

"Now that was worth waiting for," he said with a silly smile.

"I have more planned for you, but first, let's get that tea brewed." I dragged him into the house, closing the door behind him. Monty came strolling out of the living room and rubbed up against Cole's leg, purring loudly, his fur all fluffed up.

"Someone else looks like they're pleased to see you," I said.

"Hey, little fella," Cole said, bending down to pet the cat. "He's not so bad after all. Are you, fur ball?" Cole stroked him under the chin and tickled his little fat cheeks. Monty head-bumped Cole's hand, clearly enjoying the attention. I felt a little left out and hoped I would get the same kind of attention from Cole later.

"Not bad at all," Cole said, looking at me. "Ow!" he said suddenly, taking his hand away. "He bit my hand, the little…"

"He's just keeping you in check," I said, laughing as I headed into the kitchen. "Cordi, we've got another one for cinnamon rolls."

***

Cordi had helped set out the tea and the rolls on the kitchen table before retiring to the living room and leaving Cole and me alone to catch up.

I couldn't stop looking at him. Even with the bruise, he was still so ridiculously handsome. He cradled the mug of tea in his strong hands. His knuckles were swollen.

"I wouldn't like to be the other guy," I said, nodding to his hands.

He shrugged. "It's not what it looks like. I didn't hit anyone—they slammed my hand in a door when they found out Gianni and me weren't there on 'family business'."

"That sounds awful. What happened?"

"It's a long story, and I'll tell you all the details soon, I promise. I'm just glad to be back, to see you again. Alex told me what you did at Lucarelli's. That was both incredibly stupid and brave. If it wasn't for you dealing with Buttsworth the way you did, I might not still be here. That ratbag set Gianni and me up, and we didn't even suspect anything."

"He was a sneaky son of a bitch," I said, letting out the anger I felt toward Buttsworth. "But he'll likely never see freedom again. And if he does, then I doubt the Lucarellis are going to be too happy with him."

"Me neither," Cole said. "Now my cover is blown, I can't work the same anymore. The whole Robin Hood act's going to have to come to an end. I won't be able to show my face in the underworld again now that it's well known I'm a cop, or was."

"Was? What do you mean?"

He placed the mug of tea down on the table and leaned back in his chair. The wrinkles around his beautiful dark eyes that always reminded me of a young Johnny Depp creased with concern.

"I've quit the police force," he said. "I can't trust anyone there now. The corruption runs deep. I'm not going to put myself in danger like that again. Until the guys with Interpol and the Italian intelligence service turned up, I really thought I was going to die."

I put my hand over my mouth and looked away, not wanting to see the pain in his eyes; otherwise it would set me off, and if the dam broke, I'd find it hard to stop. I composed myself and said, "So what are you going to do now?" I asked. "You're not leaving, are you?"

"No," he said, reaching out and taking my hands into his. "I love you, Harley, and after what I've gone through, nothing and no one is going to take me away from you. I don't know what's next for me, but right now I just want to be with you. I'll think of something eventually, when I've healed up."

"I can help you with that," I said. "I run a great bubble bath, and I'm good with my hands."

"I'll be the judge of that," he said, leaning forward and kissing me softly. It sent shivers through me, and I felt the same electric connection from the first time we kissed. I ran my hand through his hair and held him close, exploring his delicious lips with the tip of my tongue.

Just as I was really starting to enjoy Cole being back, the doorbell went.

"I'll get it," Cordi shouted down the hall. I broke away and looked through the kitchen to the front door, thinking it was Maggie come to bring us more cake supplies. But when Cordi opened the door, I heard a male voice.

Cordi then turned to me. "Harley, it's for you." Then to the person at the door: "Please come in."

"Who's that?" Cole asked.

I shrugged. "I don't know; I best go find out."

Cole and I stood. He waited at the end of the hallway as I went to meet this new guest.

When Cordi moved aside, I recognised him immediately. "Michael!" I said, not hiding the surprise in my voice.

My brother, tall and broad, made the hallway seem to shrink with his presence. And yet, despite his considerable physical stature, I could see the bruises and cuts on his face, mirroring my experience of Cole just a short while earlier.

What was it with injured men coming to see me today?

"Sam... sorry," he said, shaking his head. "Harley, I'm sorry to drop in on you like this, but I didn't want to leave things the way they were on the phone. It all got a bit weird, and I'm sorry about that."

He was such a sweet man. How could any woman want to abuse him like this? "Please," I said, "no need to apologise. Why don't you come through and meet everyone and we can catch up properly. We've got a lot to cover."

He smiled, the tension easing from his shoulders.

As he stepped closer I could see the extent of his wounds were more considerable than I had anticipated. The familiar feeling of anger and injustice rose up inside me again. I'd barely known this man, my brother, but already I felt so protective of him.

I supposed his actions of saving me from getting squashed by a speeding car helped that. It proved he was a selfless and courageous man.

"Thank you," he said awkwardly as I showed him into the kitchen.

I introduced him to Cole and Cordi, and we all explained to him who we were and what we did. It turned out that he was a graphic designer with one of London's advertising agencies. And those children I saw him with weren't his; they belonged to his wife and her ex-husband, who had divorced her for abuse.

We talked for hours. We wept, we laughed, and we caught up with decades of lost time, filling each other in on our lives. Surrounded by Cole, Cordi, Monty, and my brother—my first real family member—I had never been happier.

Eventually as the evening settled in, I asked Michael, "So what are you going to do now, about your wife?"

He looked at me, then Cordi, with hope in his eyes. "I've left her, and well, I didn't have anywhere else to go. I was wondering if it wouldn't be too much of an imposition if I—"

Cordi cut him off, saying, "You're staying with us, and that's the end of it. Any family of Harley's is family of mine. We've a spare room that we're not using. Please, you're welcome to stay until you get things sorted."

I leaned over the table and wrapped my arms around Cordi. "Thank you," I said, "for everything. It means so much to me."

"You're more than welcome," Cordi said. "I'm just glad to see you happy and reunited with Michael."

Michael gave his thanks. He seemed embarrassed by Cordi's generosity, but we convinced him to accept her offer and stay with us a while. It would be great for him and me to really get to know each other after all these years. I was just a baby when he last saw me.

The conversations went on late into the night.

Cordi made up the spare room for Michael and showed him around the house.

I got Cole set up in my room. But before I retired for the evening and caught up with Cole properly, Michael and I were standing alone at the kitchen sink, finishing up the last of the dishes and cups, when he turned to me.

"There's something else that I need to tell you," he said. "I wanted to wait until we were alone, as I didn't know if you wanted everyone else to hear."

"You're worrying me," I said. "It's not bad news, is it?"

I'd already asked him earlier about my sisters, and he had told me that he hadn't been in contact with them since the day the photo I had of them all was taken.

"Not quite. That photo you have, with the message on the back."

"You're not alone," I said. I had stared at that handwritten note on the back of the photo for many hundreds of hours over my lifetime, wondering who wrote it and why.

"That… was written by our father."

I nearly dropped a mug to the floor. "I was always told by my foster carers that my parents… I mean *our* parents were dead."

"Harley, they're very much alive."

Thanks for Reading

Thank you for reading the second Harley Hill mystery. If you would like more information on Kennedy Chase and her books, you can find her at:

Web: **www.kennedychase.com**
Facebook: **www.facebook.com/kennedychaseauthor**

Or to get email updates of new book releases, special offers, and exclusive content, sign-up to Kennedy Chase's Mystery Parlour at: **www.kennedychase.com**